Pearl's Pork Palace

AND OTHER STORIES
FROM FLYNN'S CROSSING, N.C.

PEARL'S PORK PALACE
and Other Stories from Flynn's Crossing, N.C.

BY BILL THOMPSON

Greensboro, North Carolina
800.948.1409
ourstate.com

Pearl's Pork Palace and Other Stories from Flynn's Crossing, N.C.
Copyright © 2005 Bill Thompson
All rights reserved.
ISBN 0-9723396-8-X

Published by:
Our State Books
P.O. Box 4552
Greensboro, N.C. 27404
800.948.1409
ourstate.com

Printed in the United States by R.R. Donnelley Inc.
Cover illustration by Eric Westbrook

Publisher: BERNARD MANN
Executive Vice President: LYNN TUTTEROW
Editor & Associate Publisher: MARY BEST
Copy Editors: AMANDA HIATT AND BETTY WORK
Marketing Director: AMY JO WOOD
Marketing Assistant: DEBBIE WEST
Production Director: CHERYL BISSETT
Distribution Manager: ROBIN BIVENS

Our State
NORTH CAROLINA
BOOKS

Library of Congress Cataloging-in-Publication Data

Thompson, Bill, 1943, Sept. 18-
Pearl's pork palace and other stories from Flynn's Crossing, N.C. / by
Bill Thompson.
    p. cm.
ISBN 0-9723396-8-X (pbk. : alk. paper)
1. North Carolina--Social life and customs--Fiction. 2. City and town
life--Fiction. I. Title.
PS3620.H6525P43 2005
813'.6--dc22
                                                        2005019474

contents

❝ A small town is a place
where people care about you
whether you want them to or not. ❞
— Bill Thompson

PREFACE

As you can tell, this is a collection of short stories. Short stories, by definition, are fiction. And while the stories that follow are, indeed, made up by me, they are almost like a documentary, which, conversely, is not fiction. Much like a painting can document the image it depicts, a painting may also be viewed as an artistic expression of what the artist sees and feels and is able to convey to the viewer by use of the brush. I have tried to paint a word-picture through stories written in the first person by 10 different residents of the fictional town of Flynn's Crossing.

Flynn's Crossing is not a real town. As far as I know, there is no place, at least in North Carolina, named Flynn's Crossing. However, hundreds of small, rural communities like Flynn's Crossing do exist all across this state. Many, if not most of them, are known only to the residents or nearby residents. They are not industrial centers, but they are no longer as reliant on agriculture as they once were. Most have become "bedroom communities" to which residents return each day from jobs in more urban areas.

Many of the families who have moved to North Carolina in the last several years have sought out these communities, enjoying a relatively quiet lifestyle as opposed to the hustle and bustle of the cities in which they work. They often find that many of their new neighbors have deep roots and have chosen to stay even when they could find more lucrative employment elsewhere.

In the following stories, I have tried to portray the residents of Flynn's Crossing with some humor but also with some appreciation of their determination to remain close to their roots. Many of the stories are reminiscences of times long gone but which left an indelible mark on the lives of the narrator and, consequently, reflect the character of the individual and, by extension, the character of the town. That's important to remember because that's what a town is: a collection of people, not just buildings and streets.

Admittedly, I may have exaggerated the characters and the situations a little. But most are based on real people and situations or, more often, a composite of stories and people I have known. I'm sure there will be those who assume the activities and characters are a direct reflection of my hometown of Hallsboro. Some are, but I have drawn more on my many years of traveling across this state, speaking to civic clubs in small towns, acting as master of ceremonies for every imaginable community celebration, and getting to know the people of this great state in so many ways.

By using the words of 10 imaginary North Carolinians, I hope I have painted an interesting portrait of the small towns that constitute the heart of the Old North State. Even as we adjust to the inevitable change that comes with the progress, this collection of short stories about North Carolina life will enable us to do the remembering.

— *Bill Thompson*

" I saw Daddy give Mama a little wink as Aunt Bessie and Leon drove off in the pickup truck. I guess Daddy had some idea of what Leon had in mind and figured the bathroom might be more available soon. "

AUNT BESSIE'S WEDDING

A unt Bessie was going to get married on Saturday at the Methodist church. It was to be at 12 o'clock, high noon. She was big on tradition, and she figured a midday ceremony was the most proper kind of wedding to have. Not that Aunt Bessie followed tradition all the time. In Flynn's Crossing, women usually got married somewhere around their 21st birthday. Aunt Bessie was going on 50.

Leon McKoy was the intended bridegroom. He was not the first man Aunt Bessie had ever took up with. In fact, Mama said Aunt Bessie had run through about every eligible man in town. When I say "took up with" I don't mean she lived with them or anything like that. She might have spent the night at Mac Southern's house a couple of times and even spent a weekend at Carolina Beach with Jack McKutchin, but she said nothing happened. Aunt Bessie always said she didn't have much to offer a man but the man she married would not get any used merchandise.

Leon had been living over at Pineview Apartments and worked as a greeter at Wal-Mart. He sorta showed up last summer and next thing we knew he had joined the Lions Club and was sitting on the fourth pew from the back on the right-hand side at the Methodist church.

It was at church that Aunt Bessie met Leon. Every fifth Sunday we have a covered-dish supper and Bible study. Aunt Bessie always takes her three-bean salad. In all honesty, there weren't more than about three actual beans in her salad. There was always plenty of that salad left for her to take home but she never got the message that it was not a favorite. Leon ate some of her salad, which must have gotten her attention. I guess she figured any man who liked her three-bean salad might like her, too.

It doesn't really matter what attracted Leon to Aunt Bessie. The fact that he was the last chance she had of getting married made him most attractive to her. So when they began sitting together and singing out of the same hymnbook on Sunday mornings, we all pretty much knew what the result was going to be. The matrimonial garden in Flynn's Crossing is so small, it doesn't take much fertilizer to make it grow.

They had been going together only for a few months when Leon decided to ask for Bessie's hand in marriage. He wanted to take her someplace romantic and special so they went to Lester's Fish Camp on Saturday night. Saturday night was crab night at Lester's and he knew how much Aunt Bessie loved deviled crab. She would collect the shells, paint them different pastel colors, tie them together, and string them across her back porch for an attractive nautical effect. She told Mama it always reminded her of her trip to the beach with Jack McKutchin.

Aunt Bessie had a feeling that it was going to be a special night. She soaked in the tub for almost two hours. Ever since Aunt Bessie had come to live with us when I was real little, Daddy had said he was going to put in another bathroom. He said one bathroom and two women in a house was cruel and unusual punishment for a man. Daddy came home that afternoon when Aunt Bessie was soaking in the tub and told her she had to get out of there or he was going to come in there and embarrass her because he had been eating watermelon that afternoon and nature was calling. Aunt Bessie was out in about 30 seconds.

Aunt Bessie was really a good-looking woman for her age and when she worked at it, like she did that afternoon, she made a good impression. Mama said Aunt Bessie's hair was strawberry blond but Daddy said it was red. Earlier that afternoon she had gone down to Marie's Beauty Emporium to get her hair done and then had wrapped her whole head up in tissue paper while she was soaking in the tub and didn't undo it (the tissue paper, that is) until she had applied enough makeup to put Tammy Faye to shame. Then she put on a peach-colored sundress that clung to her body. Aunt Bessie was not a skinny woman by any means. She was curvy without being heavy. Daddy said she was on the verge of plump. I thought that was pretty diplomatic of Daddy.

She wore a pair of high-heeled shoes that were really just a bunch of straps. I heard her tell Mama that she bought them because they made her behind look perky. I never could figure out the connection between high-heel shoes and perky behinds but what would a 10-year-old boy know. I didn't even know what a perky behind was.

When Leon came to pick up Aunt Bessie, he came to the door and knocked. The first time he had come by to get her, he blew the horn but Aunt Bessie didn't come out.

When he finally came to see what was the problem, she told him that a gentleman always came to the door to get a lady when they were going out. So on that special evening Leon knew to come to the door to get Aunt Bessie.

I saw Daddy give Mama a little wink as Aunt Bessie and Leon drove off in the pickup truck. I guess Daddy had some idea of what Leon had in mind and figured the bathroom might be more available soon.

I heard Leon's truck when he brought Aunt Bessie home that night and when the front door closed she called Mama into the kitchen.

"Carlene, he asked me to marry him and I said yes. Look at this ring."

"My word, Bessie, he must make a lot of money greeting people at Wal-Mart."

"He told me he has made some good investments. He works at Wal-Mart to have something to do. He said we were going to Florida and live in a trailer park he has at Daytona Beach. Oh, Carlene, after all this time I have finally met a man who will take me away from Flynn's Crossing and give me a home of my own. Isn't it just wonderful!"

I couldn't hear all the rest of that conversation but I could tell Mama wasn't quite as excited about the announcement as Aunt Bessie. But it didn't dampen Aunt Bessie's enthusiasm. I know that the next day she went back to Marie's Beauty Emporium and showed everybody there her ring. I always figured that as long as Marie's was open, the newspaper office would have limited circulation. So it wasn't long before everybody in town knew about the upcoming wedding.

DADDY HAD MIXED FEELINGS about the whole thing. On the one hand, he was glad to see Aunt Bessie getting a husband and moving out of the bathroom. On the other hand, he was concerned about how much this wedding was going to cost him. You see, Aunt Bessie had never had a job other than little part-time jobs like wrapping packages at Belk during Christmas. She had lived with us and helped Mama take care of the house while Mama taught school. Their daddy, my granddaddy, had died when they were small and their mother had raised them by herself. When she died shortly after Mama and Daddy got married, Aunt Bessie came to live with us. So Daddy was going to have to play the role of father of the bride.

He watched with wonder as they began to plan the wedding. Mama said she could use her wedding dress. She had stored it in the cedar chest and left it in the attic. Mama said although it had been wrapped in plastic and placed in that chest it had yellowed a little. Daddy said it was appropriate that Aunt Bessie's wedding dress was a little bit off-white.

Despite Daddy's concern about the propriety, there was never any doubt that the wedding would take place at the Methodist church with the reception in the fellowship hall. Mama and Daddy had been married there so it naturally followed that Aunt Bessie would get married there, too. Daddy was glad that church members didn't have to pay any rent for weddings. Having it there also settled the question of whether or not any alcoholic beverages would be served. That would save some money. Of course, some of the guys would always have a little something to put in the punch even at the church. Daddy said ginger ale and pineapple juice taste better with a little bit of vodka. That's what gives "punch" its name, he said.

Daddy was also glad they were having the reception at the church. Mama had said something about having it there at the house but Daddy said he didn't want to have to load up all the folding chairs and tables from the church and then haul them back and forth. The church council had said nobody was supposed to do that anymore anyway since the stuff had about got worn out from being used for family reunions and such. Miss Lillie Belle Tomlin had threatened to sue the church when one of the folding chairs broke when she sat in it at homecoming. I think her lawyer told her that the chair wasn't made to hold 300 pounds and she didn't have a case, so she decided not to pursue it.

Daddy's biggest worry was Clara Mae Parker. Aunt Bessie had asked her to direct the wedding because Clara Mae was considered the authority on weddings and other social occasions. She had even been able to come up with the proper procedure and protocol when she directed J.B. Connor and Lucille Windsor's wedding on the pier down at the lake. By using the bait-and-tackle shop as a little chapel when the thunderstorm came up she was able to give some dignity to an otherwise tacky affair.

Clara Mae had talked Aunt Bessie into keeping the wedding party as small as possible. She said given Aunt Bessie's age and all, it wouldn't seem proper to have a big retinue. Nobody knew what a retinue was but if Clara Mae said it was supposed to be small that's the way it would be. Anyway, she decided to have Mama as her only attendant and Daddy to walk her down the aisle. They changed the wedding from Saturday to right after worship service on Sunday morning. Daddy was glad to see Clara Mae being so cost-conscious.

Mama and Aunt Bessie spent a lot of time making sure all the family got invitations. My great-aunt Melba was the family historian so Mama called her to get a list of all the living relatives on her side of the family, and Daddy got out his mama's Bible and looked up all the relatives on his side of the family. It turned out to be just about everybody in town. Seemed our folks didn't travel far to find a spouse. 'Course, a lot of the younger ones had gone off and married elsewhere, but they wouldn't be coming back for a wedding anyway.

During all this planning and talking about the wedding we didn't see a whole lot of Leon.

Maybe two or three times a week he'd come by and pick up Aunt Bessie and they'd go somewhere but, generally speaking, he seemed kind of in the background. One Friday night during the fall he asked me to go with him and Aunt Bessie to the high-school football game. I went with them, but Leon seemed kind of detached. He didn't cheer when we scored a touchdown or nothing and he even gave me $5 to buy a box of popcorn and never asked for the change.

I thought we'd see more of him and get to know more about him, but he never did seem to want to talk much about himself. He was real good at getting other folks to talk about themselves though. Every time Daddy asked him something about where he'd been and what he'd done, he'd start talking about Daddy's work at the hardware store. 'Course, Daddy was always willing to talk about saws and wrenches and stuff.

One night Mama had invited Leon to have supper with us and we were all sitting around the table eating and talking and Mama said something about how much she liked to listen to Lawrence Welk on television. Then Aunt Bessie said she wouldn't mind if the Big Bands came back to being popular.

Leon said, "There'll never be another time like the Big Band era. Those were shining times gone forever."

Aunt Bessie asked, "Why not, Leon? If there were enough people like us and we bought their records don't you think there'd be more bands?"

Leon didn't say anything right away, just looked up with his fork between his plate and his mouth. "Oh, I guess so," he said. "What we need is more of those tape players like you got down to the store, Charles. How they selling?"

Of course, Daddy went into how he was expanding his small-appliance business because of the decline in the hardware sales. He said he thought he'd specialize in televisions and radios and he'd certainly take a look at expanding the audio equipment like tape players.

I noticed Leon wasn't really listening to Daddy. He seemed to be thinking about something else maybe a long way off and a long time ago.

Aunt Bessie and Leon had set their wedding date for the week before Christmas. I didn't think that was a good idea since it might make folks give them fewer wedding presents what with Christmas presents coming up and all. But that didn't seem to be a problem for them. I also figured that this year Aunt Bessie wouldn't be wrapping presents at Belk since she would still be getting ready for the wedding. But she was down there every day cutting paper and taping and tying. She told Mama she wanted to make enough money to give Leon a special Christmas present. Mama asked her about her wedding present but Aunt Bessie said she was giving him the most valuable thing she had for a wedding present and winked at Mama.

ABOUT A WEEK BEFORE THE WEDDING, Leon left town. He didn't tell anybody, not even Aunt Bessie, where he was going. He said he was going to be gone for a few days but he'd be back in plenty of time for the wedding. Mama said it was awfully inconsiderate of him to leave Wal-Mart at such a busy time of year. I didn't figure they'd miss him a whole lot, to tell you the truth.

Daddy told Mama he wouldn't be surprised if Leon hadn't skipped the country. Daddy said he couldn't figure why a man with no obligations and no reason to tie himself down would want to be married. That set Mama off.

"Why, Charles Holden, you mean to tell me you wouldn't get married to me again if you found out we weren't legally married?"

Daddy could tell he had gone and said the wrong thing and started backing water. "No, honey! I was referring to Leon. I was thinking about his particular circumstances and all. You know he don't make much money working to Wal-Mart and you know Bessie is gonna be high maintenance. What I meant is I guess I ought not to be too surprised that he might want to go off and think about things before he's too far gone."

"Too far gone!" Mama said. "Listening to you you'd think the man was afflicted with some fatal disease! Did it ever occur to you that he might love Bessie?"

Then Daddy really messed up. He didn't answer right away, like he had to think about the question some more.

"Well, Charles, if you think my sister is gonna be such a burden, why don't you tell Leon to stay wherever it is he's gone to?"

By then Daddy could tell he had dug himself a hole and there wasn't any way out except to convince Mama that he was all in favor of the wedding and what a lucky man Leon was.

"Well, honey, I'd tell him how proud I was to have him become a member of the family if he was here right now. 'Course, since he's not I'll have to wait and tell him that if Bessie is half the woman her sister is he is the luckiest man on earth." Then he came up behind Mama and put his arms around her and snuggled the back of her neck. That's when I went outside.

Aunt Bessie was sitting outside on the porch swing. I don't know if she had heard any of Mama and Daddy's discussion, but I could tell she had been crying. I went over and sat down on the swing with her. "What's the matter, Aunt Bessie?" I asked.

"Nothing, Willie," she said. "It's just that I was sitting here wondering what a man as fine as Leon sees in a woman like me."

I started the swing to swinging and tried to think of something. Then I realized she probably wasn't expecting an answer from me anyway.

She went on, "I know I'm way past my prime in the looks department and I don't have any money. Your mama got all the looks in the family. And unlike me, she's smart being a teacher and all."

Then for some reason I'll never understand, I said the dumbest thing. "Maybe Leon likes you 'cause y'all so much alike."

Well, Aunt Bessie reached over and hugged me and I thought her bath powder was going to suffocate me. "You are so special, Willie," she said. "I'm going to miss you something terrible. I want you to be sure and come to visit me and Leon down in Florida." We sat there and swung for a while 'til the December chill made us go inside.

Leon came back to town on the Thursday before the wedding. Everybody had started to wonder where he was by then. Leon didn't just come back, though. It was right after supper and Daddy was fixin' to watch "Wheel of Fortune" on television. He always watched that show 'cause Mama said we needed to give Vanna White moral support, her being from North Myrtle Beach and all, which was down the road from us.

Leon arrived at the house in a new Cadillac. He drove up on the two little strips of concrete that made up our driveway and got out wearing one of those double-breasted suits. I noticed it was like the one Pat Sajak was wearing.

Nobody said anything as he walked in the door without knocking. Mama never did like anybody to do that. She said it was impolite. But she was so surprised by how Leon looked it didn't seem to bother her.

Leon went over and gave Aunt Bessie a little kiss on her cheek and then sat down beside her on the couch. Nobody had said a word.

"I guess y'all wondering where I've been," said Leon. "Well, I guess I owe all of you an explanation. I say I owe it to all of you because if I'm going to be a member of this family, I need y'all to trust me."

Then he paused a little while and took Aunt Bessie's hand and leaned back on the couch.

What followed was a story that could have been right out of one of Aunt Bessie's soap operas. Leon said he was a wealthy man. He had made a lot of money building trailer parks all over Florida. He had been married twice before but he found out that both women were more interested in his money than they were in him so he gave them a bunch of it and sent them on their way.

But he wanted to find a good woman to share his life and figured if he went to a small town where nobody knew about him or his money, he'd have a better chance of finding the right woman. "I found her right here in Flynn's Crossing," he said, looking at Aunt Bessie.

When he finished, still nobody said anything. Daddy sat there with his mouth open and Mama was crying and Aunt Bessie was crying and I was wondering how much that Cadillac cost.

Finally Leon said, "Bessie, will you still marry me?"

And she said yes.

Aunt Bessie and Leon got married that Sunday and took off for Florida by way of some place in Mexico I never heard of. That was 10 years ago and Aunt Bessie calls me every year and wants me to come down and spend part of my summer vacation with them. I always go. They don't live in a trailer park.

❝ Then the reverend said something that
I have remembered to this very day. 'All
music is good because the Lord gave us
the ability to make it. It's how we use it
that determines whether it's sinful or not.' ❞

THE VOICE OF DIXIE

Dixie had asked Mama if I could go with her to the singing at the schoolhouse that night.

She said I could. 'Course, Mama wouldn't ever tell Dixie "no" about anything. You see, Dixie had been taking care of me since near 'bout the time I was born. Not that Mama didn't want to take care of me herself but something happened to her when I was being born that made her so weak she never got over it. Daddy built a room onto the side of the house, and Dixie came to live with us.

The only time Dixie'd leave me with Mama and Daddy was sometimes on Sunday afternoons when she'd go to her church, Bethel A.M.E. Zion, which was about a mile down the road from our house. But even then, every once in a while she'd take me with her.

I liked going to Dixie's church. It was full of music, and people acted like they were glad to be there. Dixie said everybody was "rejoicing in the Lord." I rejoiced with 'em. They didn't sing out of hymnbooks like we did at the Presbyterian church, and I believe they must have had a different kind of organ 'cause the music didn't sound anything like what Miss Elsie McCall played at the Presbyterian. When Dixie sang she clapped her hands and moved that big body of hers to where she'd take up most of the pew.

It was that kind of singing that was going to take place at the schoolhouse that night. The Cooper Family and Leola were coming for a concert of gospel music. Dixie said it was not only a concert. She said it was as much a worship service as if it was being held in the church. Dixie said when you sing the Lord's music, it's a worship service no matter where you are. They were having it at the schoolhouse 'cause they figured their little church wouldn't hold the crowd they were expecting.

So we left the house about dusk-dark that Saturday night and started walking to the schoolhouse. I was carrying a plate of deviled eggs and Dixie had a pot of butter beans still hot from the stove. Every time her church had a gathering, they had a meal.

Dixie took her umbrella with her. If anybody else had taken an umbrella that night I would of thought it was a wasted effort, but Dixie never left the house without hers even in the middle of a sunshiny day. She said it would keep the sun off her sensitive skin during the day and the water off her when it rained.

I liked walking with Dixie. She smelled like soap and dusting powder and she didn't walk so fast that my eight-year-old legs couldn't keep up with her. We could see the schoolhouse almost from the time we got on the dirt road that ran in front of our house. That night we could see the lights were on at the schoolhouse, which meant that some of the church people were already there.

The school was for grades one through 12 and the lunchroom was separate from the classroom building. The school was brick but the lunchroom was a wooden frame building and the kitchen took up one side with a serving counter between the kitchen and the area where all the tables were placed. It looked a lot like my school but my school was back toward town.

There were about 15 ladies putting food on the serving counter when we walked in. Everybody greeted Dixie and some of them spoke to me. They didn't seem to notice that I was the only white face there 'cause I had been to their church and they were used to me being with Dixie.

After a while more people came in, and pretty soon Reverend E.J. Worthington raised both his hands and asked everybody to get quiet. Then, with his hands still up in the air, he asked the blessing. Daddy said that the prayer before a meal was "returning thanks," and Mama said it was "saying grace." I never did see any difference in the prayers but somewhere toward the end of the long prayer Reverend E.J. Worthington asked the Lord to bless the food so I guess when he did it he was asking the blessing.

The food was worth blessing. There were bowls of steaming collards that had been cooked with a piece of fat meat (pork). There was fried chicken, potato salad and red ham, peas and butter beans, corn on the cob, corn bread, and pieces of fatback to gnaw on along with plenty of sweet iced tea and coffee. And lots of cakes. Chocolate with chocolate icing, yellow cake layers with chocolate icing, cakes with 13 thin layers, and pineapple upside-down cake. Those ladies could really cook and everybody ate like they enjoyed it.

While we were eating, Dixie's sister, Lola, came over and asked if anybody had heard from the Cooper Family. They had been invited to eat supper with everybody, but nobody had seen them. Dixie said they ought to send somebody into town to see if they might be looking for us. So Lola told her boy Toad (his name was Ashton but we called him Toad 'cause his big eyes sorta bulged out) to go look for the Cooper Family.

Everybody, including the menfolks, had begun to clear off the tables when we saw the lights of a car come up in front of the schoolhouse. We figured that must be the Cooper Family so some of the men went over to help them get set up. But the folks in that car weren't the Cooper Family. I was standing out in front of the lunchroom and I saw three white men get out of the car. Jeremiah Harris went over and shook hands with them, but I couldn't tell what they were talking about.

Dixie and Lola came over, and they were standing behind me watching the activity. "What you reckon's goin' on, Dixie?" Lola asked.

"Looks like the white men's lost. Least I hope that's all. Every time I see white folks show up where there ain't no other white folks, I figure they's lost. If they come here on purpose, that usually ain't good."

I WASN'T OLD ENOUGH to be aware of the reason for Dixie's apprehension. Those were turbulent times in the South. Every day there was news of sit-ins and protest marches and all kinds of racial conflicts. But I didn't think about those in connection with Flynn's Crossing. Things like that didn't happen in our little town.

After a few minutes the whole group started walking over to where we were in front of the lunchroom. Dixie said, "They ain't smilin' but they ain't frownin' neither. I guess that's a good sign."

It had begun to rain and I could hear a little bit of thunder in the distance. Jeremiah was talking as he walked, "Y'all come on in out of the rain and get a bite to eat. Lola, get 'em some plates and something to eat with. Y'all help yourself. They's plenty."

Lola went back to the kitchen to get the paper plates and plastic forks. Dixie motioned for Jeremiah to come over to where she was. "Who's those men, Jeremiah?" she asked.

"They's musicians," he answered. "They said they suppose to be playing here tonight. I told 'em we had a gospel group coming. They said they played bluegrass with a little bit of gospel. They don't know what they going to do so I told 'em to eat while they was thinking. They probably are suppose to be to the white school."

"You know something, Jeremiah. If Toad don't get back here pretty soon we might have to listen to some bluegrass gospel. Folks come here tonight to hear the gospel sung. We didn't specify how that gospel was goin' to be sung. What do you think?"

"I think it's rainin' and Toad ain't much for gettin' wet and if the Cooper Family ain't here shortly, we gon' have some upset folks. It's near 'bout 8 o'clock. These folks is here. The Cooper Family ain't here. The bluegrass folks ain't gon' want to try to get to the white school at night in the rain on roads they don't know. Why don't we ask this band if they want to play for us?"

Jeremiah went over to the table where the bluegrass folks were eating supper. "You know, that rain gettin' awful heavy out there. Y'all gon' try to get over to the white schoolhouse in this mess?"

"I ain't real anxious to get wet," said the tall white-haired fellow.

"Even if it is Saturday night. I already had my bath for the week."
He laughed and the others did, too, like that was the best joke they'd
ever heard.

Jeremiah went on. "Well, I ain't asked Reverend Worthington yet,
but if he was to agree, do you think y'all might be interested in playin'
for us seein' as how the Cooper Family ain't showed up?"

The four men looked at each other for a second, then the white-
haired fellow said, "Let us talk about it, and we'll let you know."

The four men bent over the table literally putting their heads
together to discuss whether they should perform or not. The silver-
haired fellow seemed to be the leader of the group. He did most of
the talking while the others just nodded in agreement with whatever
it was he was saying. Dixie had told me to sit down and eat at the
table, which happened to be right next to the white men. I couldn't
hear everything they were saying because they were almost
whispering their conversation, but I could catch bits and pieces.

"I tell ya, boys, I ain't anxious to put that pile o' junk J.B. calls a car
on the road in this rain tonight. And since it's rained like this there ain't
no tellin' if anybody's goin' to show up at the other schoolhouse. Top o'
that, I ain't sure if it's the schoolhouse where we're supposed to be
playin'. Marie never did get a written contract and she ain't spoke to me
since she found Alma Lee's lipstick in my truck seat. Anyway, if we don't
show up at wherever it is we suppose to be, we can blame it on Marie."

The short man with the greased hair said, "Well, far as I'm concerned, I don't care who we play for long as we get paid — something
we ain't had happen in some time now."

Then the silver-haired man said, "The only thing is, we don't know
no Negro spirituals and they expecting gospel music."

Another man said, "Listen, music's music and money's money. We got the music and they got the money. Let's do it."

Jeremiah had left them to talk and went over to where Reverend Worthington was talking with some of the ladies of the church. After a brief conversation, the reverend agreed to let the bluegrass band play if they would.

About that time all four of the band members stood up and walked over to Jeremiah and the preacher. "We thought about it and we are inclined to go along with your request but we got a few questions. See, we ain't never played for a — a colored audience. We don't know if this is the kinda music you'd like. And second, how much can you pay us?"

By that time Dixie and Lola and some of the other church members had joined Jeremiah and the preacher. Miranda Smith stepped up. She was a wisp of a woman who cleaned offices in the building where my daddy had his law office. She looked at the preacher and said, "I've heard this bluegrass music, Reverend Worthington. I hear it all the time on the radio down at the law building. Them lawyers listen to it all the time. It sounds pretty much like juke joint music to me."

"And you'd know about juke joints wouldn't you, 'Randa," said Jeremiah with a chuckle.

"I been known to listen to good music wherever it might be, Mr. Jeremiah Harris. Just 'cause I happen to like that music don't mean I'm sinful anymore than the music's sinful."

Then the reverend said something that I have remembered to this very day. "All music is good because the Lord gave us the ability to make it. It's how we use it that determines whether it's sinful or not."

"Well, I propose we use it for the Lord tonight," said Dixie. "Y'all do sing gospel, don't you?"

"Yep. It's bluegrass gospel but it's gospel," he said.

"There ain't but one gospel and that's the Lord's gospel. If you play His gospel we can listen," said Dixie.

"All right," said Jeremiah. "We were goin' to pay the Coopers $50. Can y'all play for that?"

"Fifty dollars!" said the silver-haired man. "Why, buddy, for $50 we'll play all night long. We don't usually get but 25 for beer joints and 35 for auditorium shows. You got a deal. We'll go get the stuff out of the car." He took about two steps, then turned around and asked Jeremiah, "That's cash in advance, ain't it?" Jeremiah said it was and the band went off to get their instruments.

IT DIDN'T TAKE LONG for the band to get set up. They didn't have any amplified instruments and but one microphone that they all sang in to. They put everything on the stage in the auditorium, which sat in the middle of the school building with a hallway open on two sides. The classrooms were on the other side of the hall and behind the stage. There was no special lighting and no decorations. When Jeremiah turned on the switch at the back of the room, the stage and auditorium were lit.

All the folks came in pretty much at the same time. After all the talking and all going on in the lunchroom they were awful quiet. I guess they didn't know what to expect.

Reverend Worthington walked up on the stage and held up his arms again just like he did when he prayed before. He said, "Brothers and sisters, we have come here tonight to worship the Lord through the celebration of His word through music. Now, these men may not sing words from the Scriptures but if we ask the Lord, He will see that they sing with His spirit. Let us pray."

Then he prayed again. He said, "Lord, as You look down on us tonight open our minds and mostly our hearts to hear this music. Let our ears receive the joy, let our minds receive the message and let our souls be lifted up just as you were lifted from this earthly prison. Bless these men who will sing. Loose their voices, give flight to their fingers, and let the words they sing reflect our lives both as we live them now and as You would have us live tomorrow and for eternity. Amen."

Dixie leaned over to me and said, "Lester, one of these days, if the Lord is good to you, you'll be able to speak like Reverend Worthington."

After the preacher had walked off the stage, the silver-haired fellow began to speak. "Folks," he said. "We do appreciate you askin' us to sing tonight. The food was good and the money is good so we hope the music will suit you. We want to kick this thing off with a little song we been singin' for years called 'Let Me Be Your Salty Dog.' Let 'er go, boys!"

What followed was good music if you like that kind of music. The banjo player took a prominent lead; the fiddle player made the bow fairly fly across the strings; the short-armed guitar player overcame his physical limitation on the giant guitar by playing it like a dobro without the slide; and the bass fiddle player closed his eyes and played like he was in his own little world.

"Let me be your salty dog or I won't be your dog at all. Honey, let me be your salty dog." Those were some of the lyrics to the song as best I remember. They didn't lend themselves to any kind of spiritual interpretation any way you looked at it.

When they finished playing the song all you could hear was the soft swishing of the funeral home fans being waved in the humid night air. I looked up at Dixie but she wasn't looking at me. She was looking at the stage with a kind of blank stare. She sat there waving her fan.

The silver-haired fellow just looked back at the audience. For about a minute nobody said anything, then he said, "Well, preacher, I don't believe that one got a blessing."

Nobody laughed. No one said anything. Nobody got up to say it was good or bad. The preacher didn't act like he had heard the fellow say anything. Then Dixie stood up. Every face turned to look at her. In the same voice she used to ask me if I had washed behind my ears she asked, "Do y'all know 'I'll Fly Away'?"

"Yes, ma'am, I believe we do," was the response.

So they began. *"Some glad morning when this life is over, I'll fly away. To a home on God's celestial shore. I'll fly away."* By the time they got to the chorus the whole place was singing. *"I'll fly away, Oh, Glory, I'll fly away ... "*

Then they sang some more. "This Little Light of Mine," "Victory in Jesus," "All God's Children Got Shoes," and a bunch more. The whole auditorium was like a Sunday morning service at Dixie's church. Some people had stood up and were clapping their hands. Others were lifting their hands up just like the preacher had done.

AFTER A FEW OF THOSE, the bandleader said they needed to take a short break to get their breath but the audience wanted to go on. So Reverend Worthington asked if there was anybody who would like to sing a "little interlude," as he called it, while the band took a break. Well, before I knew what was happening, Dixie had me by the hand and was pulling me down the aisle toward the stage. While we were heading down that aisle she was saying, "I been takin' this boy to church with me since he was in diapers. I been readin' the Bible to him and I been singin' the songs to him. I been tryin' to think of some way to find out if any of that has been sinkin' in. Well, ladies and gentlemen, tonight's the night."

I had never been in front of a group of more than four people in my life and that was at my birthday party. This wasn't a birthday party. Dixie walked out on that stage with my hand in hers and whispered to me, "It's all right, Lester. We gonna do what we done settin' there to the kitchen table. You okay?"

I was so nervous I could hardly speak but it came to me that we weren't at the kitchen table so I told Dixie, "At the kitchen table we sittin' down." So we sat down. Dixie placed her big black pocketbook on the floor and somehow or other managed to get her body to sit on the edge of the stage, her legs hanging over. Then she pulled me down beside her.

So there we were. I'm sure that everybody in that auditorium thought the sight most unusual. There was this big black woman sitting on the edge of the stage with this little white boy. Then we began to sing. Dixie had taught me to sing by having me repeat every phrase after her. Then we'd go back and sing the whole song together.

She started out: *"Amazing Grace, how sweet the sound."*

Then I sang: *"Amazing Grace, how sweet the sound."*

Then Dixie sang, *"that saved a wretch like me."*

I sang, *"that saved a wretch like me."*

And it went on like that 'til we sang all the verses, then we sang the song together. Dixie had a booming voice but when we sang that night she kept it soft so I could be heard. My little-boy soprano voice blended with her velvet alto. The sound and the scene were special, and it made a real impression on everybody there.

We had just finished singing and we heard the sound of a banjo slowly playing that song one note at a time. Then the fiddle came in, then the guitar. Then everybody in the auditorium began singing "Amazing Grace." It was soft and slow but full, and some of the ladies were singing a little obbligato that soared above the chorus.

When the song was over, Reverend Worthington came up on the stage. He didn't raise his arms like he had done before. He just stood there for what seemed like a long time. Then he finally said, "Brothers and sisters, we came here tonight to worship and so we have. To raise our voices again would demean the experience we have all shared. This humble auditorium is now holy ground because God's spirit is here. Let us leave here, take that spirit with us, never forget it, hold it in our hearts as we remember all who shared this night with us."

And so they all left the auditorium. Nobody said a word. Jeremiah was going out the door when the gray-haired fellow stopped him. He said, "Here's your money back, friend. We owe you, not the other way around." He turned and walked away before Jeremiah could answer him.

Dixie and I started walking home. It was drizzling rain but Dixie's umbrella kept us from getting wet. Dixie hadn't said a word since we walked off the stage. I asked, "Dixie, did we do something wrong? Didn't nobody applaud and they all left the building crying."

"No, child. We didn't do nothing wrong," she said. "Now, you mind what the Reverend E.J. Worthington said. You remember what happened tonight."

THE NEXT MORNING, I rode to the Presbyterian church with Daddy. As usual there was a group of men standing out in front before the preaching service was to begin. Daddy walked over to them.

"Mornin', gentlemen," he said.

"Mornin', Henry," they all said in unison. "We were just talking about the terrible thing over to the black church last night. I didn't think anything like that would happen here. I thought that was something going on down in Mississippi and Alabama."

"What happened?" Daddy asked.

"Why, the church was burned to the ground last night. Nobody called the fire department and all that's left this morning when the preacher got there was ashes and some bricks. Terrible thing."

Daddy didn't say a word, just turned around and got in the car. We drove straight over to the Bethel church. He was looking for Dixie. He found her standing with a group of women in the ashes of the church.

"I'm so sorry, Dixie," said Daddy.

At first Dixie didn't say anything. Then she looked at Daddy and said, "Why would anybody want to burn down the Lord's house, Mr. Henry? It wasn't no 'colored' church. It wasn't no black church or Afro-American church. It was God's church. Did they think they could take God away from us by burnin' down His house?"

"Hate is a terrible thing, Dixie," said Daddy. "It's not logical."

Dixie turned away from me and Daddy and walked back over to the group of women. Daddy stood there awhile looking at the little whiffs of smoke still coming from the ashes. After a few minutes we got in the car and went home.

We didn't go back to the Presbyterian church that Sunday.

Things seemed to change in Flynn's Crossing after the fire. There weren't any protest marches or anything like that, and other than a story in the local paper not much was said about what happened. The

Bethel congregation started meeting in the school auditorium but Dixie didn't take me with her to the services. The black folks and the white folks didn't seem mad at each other but they didn't seem as friendly as they had before.

The sheriff said they would find the people who set the fire, but we didn't hear about any progress in the investigation.

School started back that fall. Daddy said it looked like the schools were going to have to integrate, which I found out meant the black children and the white children would go to the same school. But he said it would be a while yet.

Daddy bought a new Philco television before Thanksgiving. We enjoyed watching the shows but Mama said I couldn't watch much of it 'cause it would ruin my eyes. Daddy said it would ruin my mind. But I did watch the news with Daddy and I saw all the fighting among the blacks and whites in Mississippi and heard Mama and Daddy talk about how it could happen here.

The congregation had almost finished rebuilding their church and Daddy had helped them get a loan at the bank and arranged for a grant from a foundation that he was legal counsel for in Charlotte. After doing the best they could, the sheriff still hadn't found out who burned the church. In fact, his investigation had decided it must have been faulty wiring that started the fire. Some folks, particularly the church members, disagreed. But there was nothing they could do.

Just about every night when I'd watch the news I saw pictures of large groups of black folks gathered somewhere. They almost always sang a song I had never heard. "We shall overcome. We shall overcome someday," was what they sang.

Dixie had a television in her room, too. It was a little black-and-white set with a pair of rabbit ears for the antenna. Sometimes I watched it with her. Our favorite program was "The Lone Ranger." I knocked on the door of her room one Saturday night and asked if I could come in.

"Sure, child. Come on in," she said.

"Whatcha watchin', Dixie?" I asked.

"Well, it ain't 'The Lone Ranger,' honey. It's a news story about this church that was bombed down in Mississippi. Little girls was killed in it."

"Was it a church like yours?" I asked.

"Oh, the building is a lot like ours but a building ain't a church nohow. The church is where the Lord lives, honey."

"I thought the Lord was in heaven?" I said.

"Oh, yeah. The Lord's in heaven all right but He's here, too. You remember that night we sang down to the school auditorium? God was there just as sure as He reigns in heaven."

"How come we don't sing no more, Dixie?" I asked.

Dixie didn't answer. After a while she said, "You know what, Lester? We ought to sing. Let's sing right here." So right there in Dixie's little room we started to sing just like we did at the school auditorium.

While we were singing, the crowd on television started singing, "We Shall Overcome." But I didn't hear them. Instead, I heard an old black woman and a little white boy singing "Amazing Grace" with a bluegrass accompaniment played by a quartet of old white men with a black congregation singing backup.

“ But above the storm's clamor I could hear
a faint sound of a piano. At first I thought
maybe the wind had blown out a window
and was somehow making the piano keys
move. Then I realized that was impossible. ”

3

JUST BETWEEN ME AND MARY LEE

I knew there was going to be a storm way before I heard it on the radio. Even with all that newfangled radar stuff, your best weather forecasters are still the animals. They start looking for shelter and they get quiet. The chickens don't cluck and the pigs don't grunt. The cows'll start walking toward the woods at the edge of the pasture and when they get there they'll bed down.

'Course, you can't always tell if it's going to be a hurricane but there's a good chance that sometime between Labor Day and Halloween the storm will be a big one. I remember this one hurricane that came before Hazel. Hurricane Hazel seems to be the benchmark for hurricanes; for some folks it was the benchmark for more than that. It marked the time when life changed for so many people, they knew it would never be the same again.

Back before Hazel, though, we took the big storms in stride even with all the destruction they created. The one before Hazel came the fall after my wife, Mary Lee, died. She had died back in the spring. When she died I didn't feel like there was any need for me going on like I had been doing. We didn't have any children. The farm was paid for and I didn't owe anybody anything. So I had just been letting time pass uninterrupted that summer. I rented out my tobacco allotment to Mel Evans, and that money gave me all I needed for the necessities as far as I could tell. I fished a little bit down to the creek and in the farm pond. Even planned to do a little deer hunting later on that fall but I hadn't got too excited about it. Fact is, some might say I set about to grieve myself to death. So when the storm started coming up, I didn't pay it much mind.

I was sitting out on the porch that night smoking my old pipe and rocking in one of the two rocking chairs Mary Lee and I used to rock in almost every night. We'd sit out there and talk about our day's activities. Then sometimes we'd just rock and enjoy each other's company. We did that almost every night, weather permitting, for 52 years.

Sometimes, if the weather was too cold or it was raining too hard, we'd go inside and Mary Lee would play the piano. She'd never had a single piano lesson but she could make beautiful music when she struck those keys. She played mostly hymns but every once in a while she'd play some of those songs we used to hear back during the war. "Coming in on a Wing and a Prayer" was one of them. "Deep Purple" was another. My favorite was "Don't Sit Under the Apple Tree with Anyone Else but Me." She always said that was our song because she waited for me to get back from the war, and she knew I was the only one she wanted and vice versa. Mary Lee never played for anybody but me and her.

There were just a few clouds in the sky that night before the hurricane and I could see the stars shining. They looked like somebody had punched billions of pinholes in the dark sky. It was a full moon. There wasn't a bit of breeze and the September heat had eased off a little bit since the sun went down. I finished my pipe and went in to go to bed.

I left the window in the bedroom open so if a little breeze might stir it could cool the room down some. When I looked out the window before getting in the bed I saw a cloud move swiftly across the moon. Sign of high wind.

Sometime just before daybreak the wind was blowing the curtains so hard the noise woke me up. I looked outside and the sky was gray with a little misty rain. I figured the hurricane was on its way.

I went ahead and got dressed, went into the kitchen, fried me two eggs, fixed me some bacon and grits, and made me some coffee. I had learned to cook for myself since Mary Lee died but it was basic stuff. I kept it simple 'cause that's all I wanted and it wasn't hard to clean up after myself. I had kept that same old red-and-white checkerboard tablecloth that Mary Lee had made from feed sacks. It was getting a little frayed on the edges and there were some places getting thin but I couldn't bring myself to throw it away.

While I was eating I could hear the creak of the porch swing as the wind pushed it back and forth. Nobody had sat in that swing for a long time. I started to take it down one time but Mary Lee said I ought to leave it up. Somebody might come for a visit, she said. But nobody ever did. One time she said we might sit in it again like we used to when we first got married. I remember how she kinda giggled then.

I cleaned up my little bit of mess and started out to the barn. The steps leading off the back porch needed fixing. I had made the hand railing out of pump pipe so it would be good and sturdy. Mary Lee had got to where she had a hard time going up and down even those little steps so I wanted to make sure the railing was sturdy. It still was even if the steps had recently started to rot.

As I walked toward the barn I looked out across the hayfield. I had let Johnny Allen have half the cutting off that field in exchange for him doing the cutting. I didn't need a lot of hay myself since I just had a few cows and my old mule. The field was stubble now since he had cut over it about a week before.

There is something about newly cut hayfields that's comforting to a farmer even if he's not the one that did the cutting. You get a sense of completion, the end of one more season. It's the kind of feeling that can't be explained to somebody who has never gone through the process of planting and harvesting. It's not something your mind can fathom. It's something you feel in your soul.

A couple of the chickens came running up behind me. The wind was blowing their feathers backward and they clucked as they waddled toward the chicken house. I reached up on the shelf inside the chicken house and took down the bag of scratch feed and scattered it on the ground. The chickens pecked it up almost as fast as it hit the ground. Out of habit, I checked to see if there were any eggs. I found two but I left them there. Maybe the hen would come back and set on them 'til they hatched. Then I remembered we didn't have a rooster. So much for the biddies.

As I walked on around to the front of the barn, I saw little dust devils swirling across the barnyard. They danced a little while then disintegrated. I always wondered why they were called dust devils. Unlike the devil, they did disintegrate.

The barn didn't look like one of those calendar pictures you see. It wasn't even painted. The old gray boards had weathered heat and rain, and, in some places, had bowed a little and come loose from the side of the building. That meant they'd probably been green boards when we nailed them on. The tin roof had a few pieces that had rusted and some weren't attached too firmly to the rafters. The whole building leaned a little bit to the north. Nevertheless, it was as good a barn as I needed for as much farming as I was doing.

Maybelle stood inside the barn. I don't know how old that cow was but she had been around our place for a long time. Mary Lee used to get milk from her every day but she gave less and less until she eventually dried up. But we decided to keep her. Nobody would buy a dry cow, and we couldn't bring ourselves to turn her into beef.

Considering the fact that every one of her ribs showed and her hipbones stuck out like a hatrack I figured there wouldn't have been enough beef to make the slaughter worth the effort.

I CLIMBED THE STEPS to the loft and threw down some hay to the cow, then walked over to where we had cut a hole in the floor of the loft so we could throw hay down into the mule stable. Ezra, the mule, was a lot like me. We had long ago ceased to be able to work the fields. But we had such a connection there was never any doubt in my mind that the mule would be on this farm 'til he died. I had named him Ezra after Ezra Taft Benson who had been the U.S. secretary of agriculture way back when it mattered to me who held that office.

As I started back down the steps I saw a few raindrops hit the dust outside the barn door. The dust exploded in little puffs with each drop. Before I could get to the ground from the hayloft the rain had begun to come down hard and the wind had picked up. I decided to stay in the barn and wait until a break came in the storm to make a run for the house.

I picked me out a spot on some hay bales stacked over to the side of the barn. The General showed up and laid down beside me. The General was a dog that had just took up at the barn. I don't know what breed of dog he was, but I figured he had some hound in him because he did more howling than barking. He was black and white and had long ears but his hair was longer than a hound's. He was evidently the offspring of a pair who didn't discriminate in regard to pedigree, so neither did I.

The wind had picked up and I could see sheets of water blow by the barn door. The door couldn't be closed. Some time ago the hinges rusted and I never bothered to fix them. The result of that neglect was that at the moment I had an unobstructed view of the house and fields, even if a gust of wind would sometimes blow a spray of rain on me.

I could hear the wind blowing even above the sound of the rain pelting the tin roof. As I listened to that roar of wind and rain I thought about all the times I had heard people talk about how great it was to go to sleep with the sound of rain on a tin roof. This wasn't that kind of rain. This rain came down in torrents. Sometimes I could hardly see the house, which was only down the hill about 20 or 30 yards away.

But even with the noise of the wind and rain I felt comfortable and safe. I don't know why I felt safe in that rickety old barn. There were cracks in the walls, the roof leaked, and the whole place was leaning at a slight angle. But somehow I knew it was the best shelter at the time.

That notion was confirmed as I saw a piece of tin fly off the top of the house. It was a piece that was right over what Mary Lee used to call the guest bedroom. I don't know why she called it that; we never had a guest sleep in it. At one time we had thought it would be a bedroom for our children. But since we never had any, it was never used for that either. I thought I might better get to the house to see if I could keep anything in that room from getting soaked by the rain. But then I realized there was nothing in that room but a bed and a chest of drawers. By now the bedclothes and mattress were soaked and there was nothing I could do about it, so I stayed there on that bale of hay.

The water had begun to run across the barnyard and down toward the swamp. It was taking most of the barnyard with it. Gullies had already formed and the yard looked like what I pictured the Grand Canyon would look like if I was flying over it in some kind of spaceship. Tiny rivulets got bigger until they all ran together and there seemed to be one big sheet of water washing the barnyard down to the swamp. Patches of straw and leaves floated on the sweeping water, unyielding passengers on a free ride through the barnyard rapids.

Then the wind began to howl. I couldn't hear anything except the wind and the pounding rain on the tin roof. The General moved over closer to me as I watched a chicken snake slither into a pile of straw on the other side of the barn. He was looking for a dry place like we were.

Small tree limbs were being blown across the barnyard. The house sat down a slight hill from the barn, and I could see water starting to rise to the bottom step on the front and back porches. I didn't know how long the storm had been going on but it seemed a long time. The wind was relentless. The only change was an occasional gust that would blow a sheet of rain right on into the barn. There had always been a little bit of dust in the hallway of the barn but now it was dampened by the deluge.

Suddenly I heard a crash above the din of the storm. I left my perch on the hay bale and walked toward the front of the barn. I could see where a big pecan tree had fallen in the backyard of the house. I didn't know how old that tree was but it was big when Mary Lee and I were building the house. We would sit under the shade of that tree and eat our noon meal and talk about all our plans for this farm. In the fall I'd pick up enough pecans for Mary Lee to make pecan pies, the best you ever tasted.

The tree had fallen across the old well and the top of the tree had landed right on the back porch steps I had come down earlier. The well was probably gone, which was okay. We hadn't used it much in several years. Every once in a while in the summer Mary Lee would fill a gallon jar with well water, put several tea bags in it, and let it sit in the sun. Made the best tea in the world.

As I was looking at the tree, I heard an awful noise behind me and figured the barn was going to be the next victim of the hurricane. But it wasn't the wind. It was Ezra.

He had turned his heels to the stable door and kicked it down. I saw him calmly walk out into the hallway of the old barn. I guess he didn't like the idea of being shut up by himself while the rest of us were less confined. Even mules like a little company in a storm.

The old mule wasn't much to look at. I had long ago quit grooming him, so his coat was thick and patchy. I fed him well, but you could still see his ribs. There were two white spots over his withers. That was a sign of where the collar and harness had rubbed him when he was a working mule. I had kept his feet trimmed myself using an old wood rasp. Even young mules aren't pretty, and Ezra was old.

Another gust of wind blew the rain into the barn, so I retreated back to my bale. Ezra came over and started eating some of the hay. Seeing Ezra so engaged must have inspired Maybelle to do the same. So there we were: an old man and three old animals taking shelter from the wrath of a storm in an old barn.

I don't know exactly how long we stayed in that barn as the storm carried on but I remember the animals all laid down. I felt comfortable among them even as the storm swirled and howled. Every once in a while a gust of wind would blow a pecan limb across the barnyard. I saw a 50-gallon barrel rolling down toward the house, then saw that it was floating before it got to the house. The water had begun to rise some more.

I could only see one step above the water at the front porch.

I began to think about how I was going to save what was in the house. If the water kept rising it wouldn't be long before it would be in the house. Everything I had, everything that Mary Lee and I had, could be ruined or even washed away if I didn't do something soon. But I didn't know how I could save anything all by myself. I could move the furniture, but where would I put it except outside where it would still be ruined?

It's a terrible thing to watch everything you own being taken away and you're helpless to do a thing about it. But I knew there was nothing I could do and I also realized that I didn't really care. What good is having things in life if you don't have anybody to share them with? So I resigned myself to stay in that barn and watch the storm destroy my house.

THE STORM WAS STILL GOING STRONG when I thought I heard music. I would have dismissed the thought except I saw the General's ears perk up and Ezra's long ears stand upright. They both looked toward the house. The rain continued to come down as if it was coming from a mountain waterfall, and gusts of wind made waves in the rising water that lapped at the porch.

But above the clamor I could hear the faint sound of a piano. At first I thought maybe the wind had blown out a window and was somehow making the piano keys move. Then I realized that was impossible. Still the tinkling piano sounds carried across the wind.

I continued to listen, and the animals kept their attention turned toward the house. After a while the storm abated somewhat and I didn't hear the piano anymore — although the storm noise was not as loud. Then I heard the piano again as plain as day. It was no longer just a tinkling sound. I heard a melody and began to hum it and then heard the words in my mind. *"Don't sit under the apple tree with anyone else but me. Anyone else but me, anyone else but me, no, no, no …"*

I thought I was hallucinating. I had heard of people getting stir crazy in blizzards, but never in a hurricane. But the music didn't go away, and I knew I wasn't that crazy. That left only one conclusion. Somebody was playing that piano.

I began to run toward the house. The rain soaked me and the wind blew so hard I could barely walk. I slipped to the ground several times but got back up each time, determined to find the origin of the piano music coming through the howling wind. I got close to the porch and realized I was nearly up to my waist in water. I had to make my legs push through the water and the mud toward the steps.

The water was right at the top of the steps, and the boards on the porch were slick with the rain. I could hear the piano playing as I pulled myself up on the porch and stumbled to the front door. As I opened the door, the music stopped. I went over to the piano. The cover was still down on the keyboard. I could still hear the storm, but the house was dry and nothing had been disturbed. I walked through every room and the only thing amiss was the guest bedroom where the tin had blown off the roof and rain had soaked the bed. I closed the bedroom door and went to the kitchen. Nothing was disturbed.

I looked out the kitchen window toward the barn — the haven I had just left. I saw Maybelle and Ezra headed down toward the pasture where the other livestock had bedded down. The General was running toward the backyard and I shortly heard him land on the porch. I opened the door to let him in but that dog had never been in a house. He shook the water off his fur and then laid down just where the pecan tree had fallen at the edge of the porch.

Still shaken by the piano music that now was silent, I began to think of how I was going to survive. Water was on the verge of coming in the house, and the wind was still blasting away. I got some towels and put them on the threshold of the front door. I realized that was a futile attempt to stem the flow of water if it ever got that far, but I couldn't think of anything else to do.

Suddenly, I heard a tremendous crashing noise. It came from the direction of the barn.

I rushed over to the window and saw the old barn settling on its side, the roof collapsing on top of it. The safe haven of only an hour ago was now a heap of rubble.

THE RAIN AND WIND CONTINUED for another hour or so. Then the wind became infrequent gusts and the rain became a drizzle. About nightfall all was quiet. The hurricane was over.

I didn't have any electricity for a couple of days, but I got along without much problem.

Some people from the county extension office came out to check on me and I told them I was fine except I'd lost my barn. They told me they were sorry to hear that. I didn't care whether they were sorry or not but I thanked them for coming out anyway.

I spent most of the next several weeks cleaning up my place. I picked up the splintered remains of the barn and burnt most of it.

I made a small shed for Maybelle and Ezra out of what I could salvage. Never did find the chickens. I cut up the pecan tree into firewood. Everything pretty much settled back into normal.

I never told anybody about the piano music. I figured that was just between me and Mary Lee.

“ I have eaten many a pound of barbecue in
Pearl's and never regretted a mouthful. No,
sir, the food was always good and they
always priced it so everybody could afford it.
Gonna be a real loss not having a good place
to get barbecue around here. What's a town
without barbecue, you know what I mean? ”

4

THE NIGHT PEARL'S PORK PALACE BURNED DOWN

I was headed out to Charlotte early one morning when I passed by Pearl's on the way out of town. I always liked to smell the pig cooking on the big barbecue pit she had behind the little café. Pearl cooked her pigs fresh every day, starting the process shortly after midnight so the lunch crowd was assured of the freshest barbecue. But that morning I could see more smoke than usual billowing up from the building. I pulled into the parking lot, trying to avoid all the mud holes I could. As I opened the car door I saw Pearl come running out of the building shouting, "Call the fire department! My place is on fire!"

I picked up my cell phone and dialed 911, and in a few minutes I could hear the sirens of the firetrucks coming down the road. They made a valiant effort but they couldn't save the old building. In a few minutes the pit shed and the dining room were reduced to ashes. The fire chief said so much grease had accumulated on the walls of the building over the last 60 years that the place burnt like a torch. The only thing left of the pit was the cinderblock walls and the metal grating on which thousands of pigs had become the best barbecue in North Carolina.

Pearl sat down in the muddy parking lot and cried. She didn't seem to notice the crowd that had gathered or that she was only wearing her nightgown, which was soaking wet and muddy. Several folks had gone over to console her but I don't think she even heard them.

After a while she got up off the ground and walked over toward her house, which was only a few yards away. She waved everybody away telling them, "Y'all go on. I'm gonna be awright."

Pearl was a tough old bird but she seemed to have a sense of defeat right then. She had come through some tough times, both in her business and her personal life, but I had never seen her even indicate that she would give up. Until that morning.

As the neighbors and the firefighters were leaving, I went over to check on her. I didn't know what to say but I couldn't leave her there to face the disaster alone.

"Pearl, I wish there was something I could do," I said. She made no reply as she sat in an old rocking chair on her front porch. Neither the house nor the café had changed since being built right after World War II. Pearl had kept the house painted, and the little yard was neat and clean. It was a small house, just big enough for her and her late husband, Ernest, to live in. They hadn't needed a big house. They had spent almost all of their time working. They would close the restaurant about 9 every night, sleep for a few hours, then start cooking for the next day. So the house was only a place to sleep.

Ernest died about 10 years ago. He and Pearl had bought the place right after Ernest came home from the war. They had gotten married before he went overseas to fight the Japanese. Theirs was the first barbecue joint in the area. In fact, there weren't many places to eat, period. The hotel downtown had a pretty good dining room and some of the boardinghouses let non-boarders take their meals there. Avery Mitchell had a seafood shop with a place on the side where he would cook fish for a few people at a time, and Miss Eva Mae Parsons had a tea room where a few folks would eat on special occasions. So when Pearl and Ernest opened up their barbecue joint it had a lot of business.

Back then the county was made up of a lot of small farms, especially tobacco farms. When the tobacco market was open it was not unusual to see lines of people stretched all the way down to the train depot at noontime. Pearl would handle the cash register and Ernest would do the food preparation. Later on they hired some ladies to help them during the tobacco market. There were no waitresses. Folks came up to the counter and ordered, then took their food to the few tables set up or went on home. The most common take-out order was a pound of barbecue with slaw and hush puppies. That was still the most popular order the day before the fire.

I hadn't said a word for a while when Pearl finally spoke again. "I can still smell that hog a-burnin' back there. That woulda been a good one, too."

I didn't think Pearl was in the mood to talk so I turned to leave. "Where you goin', Billy Ray?" she asked.

"I got to get on to Charlotte. I'm meeting some folks there for a business lunch," I answered.

"Business lunch, huh? We used to have a lot of folks come here for business lunches. 'Course, they didn't call 'em business lunches. Most of 'em called it 'a bite to eat.' Right 'bout noontime you'd see the cars and pickups start pullin' in this ol' muddy parking lot. Durin' tobacco market we'd feed two or three hundred people in the middle of the day. Near 'bout everybody in Flynn's Crossing and their cousins. Ernest used to say that, you know. Said everybody in this county was kin. That's why he called everybody 'Cuz.'

"He'd say, 'Whatcha havin', Cuz?' and near 'bout ever' one of 'em would say, 'Pound o' barbecue with slaw and hush puppies.' Near 'bout ever' time. Near 'bout. You know how many times we took them orders, Billy Ray? Musta been a hundred thousand. Over 50 years of servin' barbecue. That's a lot of hogs, you know that, Billy Ray? Been a lot of people eat some of mine and Ernest's barbecue. Lot of the people gone now just like that old building. 'Course, they didn't burn down. Then again, some of 'em mighta burned later on." Then Pearl smiled. It seemed like the memories wiped away some of the sadness for a second.

"Like ol' Elroy Jinkins. I'll bet he burned when he died. He was the meanest man I ever knowed. He's the one what come in one night and held a shotgun on Ernest 'til he filled a tow sack full of barbecue. Told Ernest he was takin' it up to Fayetteville to the Army boys at Fort Bragg. Gonna sell it to 'em hisself. Ernest cut the meat up right there on the pit. Just cut it up in chunks. He told Elroy he could steal his barbecue but if he told them boys it come from our place he'd track him down and kill him. Told Elroy that barbecue hadn't been fixed yet, didn't have that special sauce to go on it. Said he didn't want them boys to eat that barbecue thinkin' it was his and it not done yet 'cause it'd ruin his reputation. You know, Elroy come back 'bout a week later and give Ernest a bunch of money. Said he kept his commission from the sellin' of that barbecue to the soldiers. Ernest took the money and him and Elroy sat out there at the pit and had a drink together. I told Ernest that was a hell of a way to do business."

I have a real hard time knowing what to do when women begin to weep. When I saw a tear start to run down Pearl's cheek I didn't know if I should stay and offer some comfort or leave her to her sorrow. So I asked, "Pearl, are you sure there's nothing I can do to help you?"

She didn't answer right away. She sniffed a little bit and looked over to the remains of the barbecue joint. "I want you to stay with me a little while, Billy Ray. There ain't nothin' you or nobody else can do right now but it'd be good of you to let an old woman talk to keep from crying.

"We had insurance on the building. I reckon I can build another one if I want to. But I don't know if I want to. It wouldn't be the same, and if I didn't have Ernest to help me and to share in the task I don't know if it'd be worth the effort. A new building wouldn't be Pearl's Pork Palace. It'd just be another barbecue joint. It'd be a building without a soul, you know what I mean?"

THAT WAS THE MOST I'd ever heard Pearl say all at one time. I realized that as many times as I had been in that café about the most I'd ever heard her say was, "Whatcha havin' today, Billy Ray?" But if she wanted to talk I'd listen, so I put my back up against the porch post and let her talk.

"There's been some shinin' times in that place. Time was there'd be people lined up out the door waitin' for that barbecue. Sometimes they'd get over-anxious like the time Lemuel Hicks' wife was 'bout to have that baby. It was her first one and Lemuel and Loretta couldn't afford to go to the hospital and they had called ol' lady Hatton to come to the house and midwife the baby.

"Me and Ernest had just fired up the pit to start cookin' about 3 that mornin' when Lemuel come runnin' in and said he needed a pound of barbecue, a pound of slaw, and some hush puppies. Ernest asked him what in the heck he wanted that for at that time of morning.

" 'Loretta said that baby ain't comin' 'til she had some nourishment and she hadn't eat nothing for about two days — bein' as she had been sick on her stomach and couldn't cook nothing,' he said. 'Miss Hatton said she wasn't no cook and Lord knows I ain't, so you the only place I know that's got anything to eat. Can you fix me up somethin' real quick?'

"Ernest looked at Lemuel as straight as he could and said, 'Lemuel, you know I don't serve no barbecue that's more than 24 hours old and we sold plumb out today anyway. Now, you know it takes about 10 hours to cook barbecue that's fit to eat, and I ain't even got the wood started for tomorrow's pork.'

"Well, sir, Lemuel looked like the angel of death was perched on his shoulder. He said, 'You gotta help, Ernest. My wife's ailin' and my baby ain't goin' be born if I don't get some barbecue.'

"I started thinkin' how we could help Lemuel. He wasn't just a customer, you know. He was like everybody else that come in the place. He was our friend. I thought to myself, now what kind of friend would let their friend down in a time of need? Then it come to me that me and Ernest and Lemuel and Loretta had friends scattered all over Flynn's Crossing. So I told Lemuel to wait right there and I'd be back in a little while with some barbecue.

"Well, I got in that old Plymouth that Ernest had bought when he come home from the war and I went over to Marie's house and woke her up and told her what the situation was. She looked in her Frigidaire and found a little bit of barbecue that she had left over from supper and she give that to me. Then I tried to remember who all had come in the café that night for supper, and I remembered that Clarice Bellamy and her husband had come in and got near about four pounds of barbecue to have for some of her family who was comin' in from Raleigh. So I went and woke up Clarice and she give me 'bout two pounds of barbecue and six or seven hush puppies. Then I went back to the café and added some slaw that was in the Frigidaire. When I put it all together I give it all to Lemuel and told him to take it on home.

"Lemuel never did say nothin' about that night even when he'd come into the café. But one day he come drivin' up in his pickup and he had a big ol' hog in the back of it. He had tied that hog's legs together and laid it down in the back of that truck and it was squealin' and hollerin' so you could hear it all over town. Ernest went out there and ask him what he thought he was doin' and Lemuel said he had brought him a hog. When Ernest asked him what he wanted him to do with the hog he said, 'Cook 'im.'

"Then he pulled that hog out of the back of that truck and left him laying there in the parking lot. Ernest called David Lee down at the abattoir to come and get 'im and after he cut up the hog we cooked him right there on that pit that you see over there. Lemuel was a proud man. Didn't want to owe nobody nothin'. 'Course, we had to give Marie and Clarice some free barbecue, you know."

I could see the hint of a smile creep into the edge of Pearl's mouth when she finished telling that story. Just the recollection of the times she and Ernest and the rest of Flynn's Crossing had shared seemed to ease the pain of losing the building.

She didn't say anything for a while so I figured she had talked enough for me to leave her there where she'd be all right. I said, "Well, Pearl, if there's nothing I can do for you right now, I think I better get on to Charlotte. I'll be back in a couple of days, and you know if there's anything I can do for you, all you got to do is ask. You take care now."

THAT FRIDAY AFTERNOON as I was coming back from Charlotte I drove by Pearl's and saw that there were two bulldozers pushing up the remains of the former café. There was also a guy working a front-end loader putting the charred remnants of the place into a big dump truck. I didn't see Pearl anywhere around so I didn't stop. I figured she had decided to get on with cleaning up the debris. I didn't know if she was going to rebuild or not.

I found out what was going on the next morning when I went to Ervin Hunt's barbershop to get my hair cut. Ervin's was one of those places that had refused to change. He had three barber chairs in the shop but was the only barber. The younger barbers who had talked to him about renting a chair considered themselves hair stylists and Ervin said he wasn't running a beauty shop so if they wanted to style hair instead of cut it, they'd have to find another place.

As I settled into the chair, Ervin immediately began cutting my hair and telling me about Pearl's disaster. "Shame about Pearl's place burnin' down, ain't it? I tell you, I have eaten many a pound of barbecue in that place and never regretted a mouthful. No, sir, the food was always good and they always priced it so everybody could afford it. Gonna be a real loss not having a good place to get barbecue around here. What's a town without barbecue, you know what I mean? Listen to me now. If we don't watch out some of them hamburger chains'll come in here and they'll try to sell us barbecue sandwiches that's been froze and won't that be a sad commentary on the state of food in Flynn's Crossing?"

I told Ervin I had seen the cleaning up process going on as I came into town the day before and wondered if he'd heard anything about Pearl's plans for rebuilding.

"You ain't heard then," said Ervin. "Doc Wilson came in yesterday and said that they had put Pearl in the hospital. Said she hadn't eat nothin' since the place burned down and she was 'bout to starve herself to death grievin' over the fire and all. Said they were givin' her glucose, you know, to keep her alive but she wouldn't take nourishment."

"Who's cleaning up the mess out there if Pearl didn't call them?" I asked.

"Best I can figure from what I hear, it was kind of a joint decision on the part of the town council and Junior Hicks' construction company. Seems the town said the mess had to be cleaned up, but since it was on private property they couldn't do it with town money, and Pearl wouldn't even talk about it so Junior decided to do it and figure out who was going to pay for it later."

After I got my haircut I decided to go by the hospital and see Pearl. When I got to her room she was lying flat down on the bed with a bunch of tubes going into her body. She had her eyes closed. I figured she was asleep, so I started to leave when I heard her say, "Come on in and sit down, Billy Ray."

She didn't sound weak. I figured from what all Ervin had told me that she was just wasting away waiting for death to claim her. I said, "Hey, Pearl. How ya doin'?"

"Well, evidently I ain't doin' too good or I wouldn't be here, now would I?" she said.

"I hear you're not eating. You just lost your appetite or going on one of those crash diets?" I asked, trying to sound cheerful.

"I tell you what it is, Billy Ray. Them doctors don't believe me and ain't nobody else asked me. I'm goin' through barbecue withdrawal. Billy Ray, there ain't been a day since June the first of 19-and-46 that I ain't eat barbecue. I believe that my body has got to where it knows that some time during the day it's goin' to get some barbecue. But since my place burned down, I ain't been able to get none. What I need is about a pound of real barbecue and some slaw and hush puppies and I'll be good as new.

"Now, Elmo Watts and Melba come by and I told them and they went to Wilmington and got some barbecue but it weren't the right kind. I got to have the real thing, cooked over oak wood coals and seasoned just right."

"Well, Pearl, you tell me where to find it and I'll go get it," I said.

"All right," she said. "You know where Pender's Branch is down toward the beach? You go down the main highway 'til you get to Simmons Crossroads where Montjoy's sawmill used to be and you turn left there. Go 'bout three mile down that road 'til you come to a dirt road goes off beside an ol' tobacco barn. Go down that road 'til you come to a dirt crossroads and you'll see a little place called Roosevelt's Lunchroom. It's run by a fella who used to work for me and Ernest. He knows how to cook barbecue like it ought to be. You get me a pound of barbecue with slaw and hush puppies and you will see life spring back into this old body."

NEEDLESS TO SAY, I went in search of Roosevelt's Lunchroom. I followed Pearl's directions and came out exactly where she said I would. The eating establishment was not built to accommodate many people, but I could smell the wood burning mixed with the smell of pork cooking over the coals. It was a flat-topped cinderblock building with a small double-door in the middle and a plain glass window about four-foot square on each side. The front had been painted a light blue but the side remained unpainted. A sign ran almost the width of the building proclaiming the name of the place with a Coca-Cola emblem on each end of the sign.

I could see the pit behind the building. It was open with a tin shelter built over it. Beside the pit was a man with a flattened shovel placing hot coals under a grating on which lay the split carcass of a hog.

"'Lo," I said as I walked up toward the pit. "I'm Billy Ray Walker and I'm looking for Roosevelt."

The man looked at me as he held the shovel full of hot coals. He didn't answer right away. Everybody should experience the moment of having a big man with a shovel of hot coals look at you. He looked at me a minute then placed the coals under the grating. With his back turned to me he asked, "Why you lookin' for Roosevelt?"

"A friend of mine said he made just the right kind of barbecue that she needs and she sent me to get it," I replied.

"Who your friend?" he asked.

"Lady named Pearl back at Flynn's Crossing," I answered.

"Well, sir, if Miss Pearl sent you, I'm Roosevelt. But what's Miss Pearl want with my barbecue? She makes the best they is. I know 'cause I learned from her."

I told him the story about the fire and Pearl being in the hospital and what she had said about needing the right kind of barbecue. He laughed and said, "Miss Pearl, she meant I still cook my pigs like her and Mr. Ernest taught me. I wasn't nothin' but an orphaned boy when I worked for them. I stayed in a little room in the back of the café and helped with the cookin'. I was the one who split most of that oak wood and I learned everything Mr. Ernest knew 'bout barbecue. When I got grown and married I moved down here. Mr. Ernest and Miss Pearl, they fronted me the money to build my place and every colored family in this part of the country eats my barbecue. If Miss Pearl wants some of it, she can sure have all she wants."

With that he walked into the small building through the back door.

Even inside I could still smell that wood smoke and pork smell. The kitchen was clean as a pin. He went over to a counter and uncovered a large pan of pork that had not yet been sliced up. He began to cut it, quickly turning it into that familiar form we called "chopped."

"How much she want?" he asked.

"Just a pound of barbecue, some slaw, and hush puppies is all she said," I answered.

"She gon' need this every day for a while I 'spect but she won't eat it if it ain't fresh. You take this with you and I'll bring some more every day 'til she gets everything worked out."

"How much do I owe you?" I asked.

Roosevelt looked at me like I had insulted him. I saw a little glint of anger come briefly to his face. Then he said, "Nothin'. That account done been paid in full."

I TOOK THE BARBECUE back to the hospital and gave it to Pearl. She opened the bag and smelled it first, savoring the aroma. "This is it, awright," she said. She reached in and brought out a hush puppy. She ate it quickly. Then she brought out the little cup of slaw and placed it on the small table beside her. I pulled the moveable counter up to her bed and she placed all the contents of the bag on the little table. Roosevelt had, out of habit I guess, placed a plastic fork in the bag. Pearl took the fork and loaded it with a small amount of barbecue. Then she placed it in her mouth and let it rest there. She didn't chew it right away, just closed her eyes and savored the taste of it.

"Everything is goin' to be awright now, Billy Ray. I thank you," Pearl said.

I left Pearl there enjoying her barbecue. In a few days some folks came in the bank and told me that Pearl had gone home from the hospital. They couldn't believe the remarkable recovery. They did say something about a black guy who came to see her every day.

Shortly after that I was out of town on business for a few days and when I came back I saw workmen putting up the framing for a new café where Pearl's used to be. I stopped by Pearl's house to see her and she told me that the insurance paid enough for her to build a new café.

"I thought you said if you rebuilt, it wouldn't be the same?" I kidded her.

"You never did listen too good, Billy Ray. I said if I built it back, it would be a building without a soul. But there was two things I didn't figure on. One of 'em bein' Junior Hicks. You remember me tellin' you 'bout Lemuel Hicks' wife wantin' barbecue before she could have her baby and how I rounded up some from all over town? Well, Junior is that baby. He come by the other day and said he'd help me build the Pork Palace back and not charge me for nothin' but the material. Said if there hadn't been no Pork Palace, he wouldn't of never come into this world.

"But even with that offer I turned him down 'til the second thing happened. While I was still in the hospital I got to thinkin' 'bout what I was goin' to do. Then one day when Roosevelt come bringin' me the barbecue, it come to me. So I told Junior to go ahead."

"What changed your mind?" I asked, curiosity getting the better of me.

"I ain't gon' tell ya, Billy Ray. You just walk out there to where they buildin' the new pit and you'll see."

So I did. I walked through the front of the building under construction and when I got to the back I saw an amazing sight. In exactly the same spot the old pit had been, using what remained of it, was another one under construction. And at the end of the pit, with his back to me, I saw a big man who had to be Roosevelt.

I walked over and shook his hand, asking, "What are you doing here, Roosevelt?"

"Well, after you left and I come up here to see Miss Pearl, I figured out I had done tol' you a lie."

"What was that?" I asked.

"I tol' you the account was paid in full. But it wasn't. I'm gonna build this back just like Mr. Ernest built it, and I'm gonna cook barbecue just like he done. Miss Pearl said we would be partners." Then he laughed. "She said what this place needed was some soul and I was the one to give it."

" He was so sweet I wanted to hug him and
kiss him and tell him yes. But I didn't. In
the back of my mind I still had this dream
of being a country singer and I knew that
was not what Leslie wanted his wife to be. **"**

STAND BY YOUR MAN

Ever since I can remember I have wanted to be a country singer. Every chance I got I'd buy a record by Dottie West or Loretta Lynn or Tammy Wynette. I'd listen to them over and over on that little record player Mama and Daddy gave me for Christmas when I was about 10 years old. Now, at 22, I'm still playing that music on my stereo.

I never could get into this new kind of country music like Shania Twain and them sing. That's not my idea of "country." For me a country song's got to have a heartstring and you can strum it or pluck it or slide a bow across it, but if it don't touch your heart, it ain't country.

Mama and Daddy gave me a guitar for my 15th birthday. It came with a book that told you how to play songs like "Down in the Valley." You didn't need to learn but a couple of chords and I learned them and played them so often Daddy finally said he was going to make me play them out in the packhouse.

All through high school I told everybody I was going to be a country singer. This was when everybody else was listening to Madonna and such. But I kept on listening because listening was about all I could do in Flynn's Crossing. There is not now nor has there ever been a place where you can hear live country music in Flynn's Crossing or anywhere else on a regular basis within a hundred miles. I always thought it was kind of ironic that you couldn't be any more "country" than where we lived but there was no place to sing about it.

'Course, there was one place to sing but it wasn't for country songs. I sang in the chorus when I was in high school, but most of the time Miss Eloise had us sing Broadway stuff that just didn't appeal to me. Then there was church. I been singing in the choir since I was about 13 or 14. Miss Eva Mae Mayland plays the piano and picks out the specials that we sing and tries to teach us to sing 'em. That's about the extent of my musical education.

We sing mostly hymns in the choir, of course, but every once in a while Miss Eva Mae will come up with a gospel song that comes pretty close to being country. In fact, I sometimes think that some of those new-gospel writers just took some country tunes and put church lyrics to them.

I always enjoyed the times when we'd have some gospel singing group show up for special occasions like homecoming or revival at church. As it turned out, it was one of those occasions that helped me take the first step toward reaching my dream of being a country singer.

We had revival twice a year, once in the spring and once in the fall. It was the fall revival when The Colby Family came to sing the last night of the preaching. I got to the church a little early 'cause I wanted to meet one of the members of the group personally. The bass singer was a cousin of my Aunt Lillian who lived over in Rockingham County and she had told me to give him her regards. I don't know what I really expected to see when they arrived but it was a surprise anyway.

They showed up driving a van and pulling a little trailer behind it. On the side of the van was "The Colby Family" written up in a swirly kind of print and then the same thing was written on the side of the little trailer. I figured the trailer was what they hauled all their instruments in. Boy, was I surprised to see that it didn't have a single guitar, fiddle, or any other musical instrument in it. It was packed to the gills with sound equipment: big speakers, little speakers, microphones and microphone stands, and a great big desk-looking thing that had about a hundred dials on it.

Now, our church is not all that big, and I don't know why they thought we were all hard of hearing bad enough to need all that much amplification. When they got through unloading and setting it up in the front of the church it filled the whole place up to the point that they had laid a piece of plywood across the baptismal pool and had put two great big speakers up there. It was a good thing there was no water in the pool 'cause it could have been dangerous with all that electrical stuff sitting over it.

Since I didn't want to slow them down any while they were setting up I waited until I thought they were through to find out which one was Aunt Lillian's cousin. So I asked the short fellow with the slicked-back hair which one was David Kelsey and he pointed out the fellow who was sitting behind that great big desk with all the dials. I went over and introduced myself. "Hello," I said. "I'm Louise McCain, Lillian McCain's niece. She wanted me to meet you and to give you her regards." He reached out and shook my hand and told me he was pleased to meet me. Then I guess my curiosity got the better of me and I had to ask, "Are y'all an a cappella group? I don't see any instruments anywhere."

He laughed and said, "Oh, no. We use accompaniment tracks."

"Accompaniment tracks? What's that?" I asked.

"They're recordings of the songs we sing with all the instruments but without the vocals. It allows us to have a full sound without having to have a lot of musicians travel with us.

"It saves a lot of money without giving up any of the quality of the performance. I run this soundboard here that plays the tapes and the singers sing along as if there were real instruments playing with them. Everybody's doing that nowadays since it's so hard to find and keep musicians."

Accompaniment tracks! Who woulda ever thought it! Just like singing along with songs on the radio but without the singers. As the singing went along that night I was amazed.

The whole performance sounded like a concert on television instead of a group of people singing at little Flynn's Crossing Freewill Baptist Church.

FOR THE NEXT SEVERAL DAYS, I kept thinking about that singing with accompaniment tapes. It got to where I was so distracted I didn't pay attention to what I was doing at work. I was glad to have a job as a cashier at the Piggly Wiggly and Mr. Washam, the store manager, had already told me that he was considering me for assistant manager. But he called me aside just before we closed on Friday night and asked, "Louise, what ails you? Your register ain't checked out right for the last two days. I know it ain't because you takin' any money because the mistakes are in the store's favor. This ain't like you. You ain't concentrating. Did you and Leslie break up?"

That was a logical question for Mr. Washam to ask about me and Leslie. Leslie Carter and me had been going together since high school. In fact, he was the only boy I ever dated and we (and everybody else in town) kind of assumed that one day we would get married. He had a good job over to Lowe's in the paint department. He had bought him a new doublewide trailer and set it up on his daddy's place outside town, and we figured it wouldn't be too long before we'd get married. Fact is, Leslie had asked if I wanted to go on and move in with him since I was still living with Mama and Daddy and we didn't have enough privacy. I really didn't want privacy for the same reason Leslie did and that caused us to have some disagreements from time to time. But that wasn't the cause of my distraction at the store.

So when Mr. Washam asked me what was going on with me I felt like I owed him an explanation. "Well, Mr. Washam," I said. "It's all about taped accompaniment. That's what I got on my mind and I just can't seem to think about nothin' else."

Mr. Washam didn't say anything. He just looked at me and blinked his eyes like the light was bothering him. Finally he said, "Taped accompaniment." Then there was another long interval where he just looked at me. I figured he needed a little further explanation so I said, "Yes, sir. I heard a gospel group sing with taped accompaniment and it was like a revelation to me. Not the music — although it was wonderful — but the fact that they were singing without any instruments and it was like they were at the Grand Ole Opry or somewhere. There was guitar music and fiddle music and trumpets and a piano and all that, but it was on a tape — just like you play here in the store except prettier."

After another minute of silence Mr. Washam said, "Louise, I know you've had a lot on your mind lately what with Leslie and your mama and them. Why don't you take tomorrow off and rest a little bit. I'll pay you just the same. Then when you come back Monday I'll bet you won't be so addled."

So I did. I didn't go to work that Saturday and sometime about the middle of the morning Leslie called. He'd heard that I hadn't showed up for work at the Piggly Wiggly and he wanted to know if I was all right. Leslie is real thoughtful like that. I told him I was fine, so he then asked if I wanted to go over to the Rainbow Fish Camp for supper that night. Well, we always got together every Saturday night for supper so I told him I'd like that. He said he'd pick me up about 7 o'clock.

I spent the rest of the day helping Mama clean up around the house and thinking about accompaniment tracks. I wondered where The Colby Family got them. Did they go into a recording studio and pay a bunch of musicians to record for them? How much would that cost? Where there a recording studio besides Nashville?

When Leslie came to get me and I got in his pickup, I slid over close to him like I always did. He gave me a little peck on the cheek, and we started out for the fish camp. I felt comfortable with Leslie. We had been a part of each other's lives for so long, being with him seemed like a natural thing. I shared everything with Leslie except for one thing. I believe Leslie thought I'd share that, too. That was why he kept saying we needed more privacy. That was his way of saying he wanted me to go to bed with him. But that wasn't going to happen and he knew that. Since this accompaniment track thing had been on my mind so much, I began to tell Leslie about it.

"Oh, yeah," he said. "I've heard about that. All the big stars use 'em sometimes when they make guest appearances on television and such. I heard Jay Leno talking about it the other night when Jessica Simpson was on his show. She used tracks."

I wasn't surprised to know that Leslie had watched Jessica Simpson. Ever since we had seen her at the Azalea Festival in Wilmington I knew he was a fan. He was smart enough to tell me I looked like her. I was smart enough to know that I didn't, but even Leslie deserved a little fantasy given his lack of privacy. Talking about watching television led Leslie to tell me that he had just bought a big-screen television to go in his doublewide.

"After supper I'll show it to you," he said.

When we got to the Rainbow Fish Camp there were a whole lot more cars and trucks parked there than usual. I looked at Leslie and he smiled and said, "This is a special night. Larry Grainger told me that the Carolina Ramblers were playing tonight and we had to have tickets to get in. So I bought us two. Just thought I'd surprise you."

The Carolina Ramblers is one of my favorite bands because they sing the old-time country music. I was so excited, I reached over and hugged Leslie and kissed him right on the mouth. I didn't let the kiss last too long 'cause I wanted to go on in the fish camp, but I could tell Leslie was very pleased with my response.

We gave our tickets to the boy at the door and he told us we had special seats to the right of the stage. The band wasn't there yet but everything was set up. We took our seats and ordered. I got fried shrimp and oysters and Leslie got the seafood platter. We had almost finished eating when Larry Grainger came out on the stage and introduced the band. They got a big round of applause and immediately began to sing. I loved it. There were six of them: a lead guitar player, a bass player, a drummer, a keyboardist (since it's hard to tote a piano around), a fiddler, and a fellow on steel guitar — the perfect country band.

When they started to play a slow song, Leslie asked me to dance. He wasn't much of a dancer so about the only time we danced was when the band played a slow song. I'm not much of a dancer either but I like Leslie holding me close. Neither one of us had ever had anybody teach us to dance. We just put our arms around each other and swayed to the music. I was so caught up in the dancing that it took me a minute to realize there was a trumpet playing and not just one fiddle but a bunch of violins. I stopped dancing and looked to the band to see if some more people had come in. But there were the same six people and the same six instruments. Before I could figure it out, the music ended and we went back to our table.

But I couldn't get the mystery of the trumpets and violins out of my mind. I asked Leslie and he said I ought to know by now that the band was using accompaniment tracks to add to some of the songs. Accompaniment tracks. Here they were again. I was not shocked, but I was disappointed because I hadn't realized the music wasn't actually being played live. I still enjoyed the show and when we went back to Leslie's later I asked him how he knew about accompaniment tracks.

"Some of the sound equipment we sell at Lowe's is what they call 'singalong' machines. It's got a tape player hooked up with a microphone and you can just sing along like you was singing with a band," he said.

"Will you show me some time?" I asked.

"Sure," he said.

We started watching a show on Leslie's new big-screen television. As usual he talked about our need for privacy. I told him I had been thinking a lot about what I was going to do for the rest of my life. I told him I had dreamed of being a country singer all my life and if I was going to pursue that dream I needed to get on with it. I told him that my learning about these accompaniment tracks might be the revelation God was giving me to show me how to reach my dream. I told him that if I could get hold of some tapes I could perform anywhere. All I needed was one of those singalong machine things and a place to sing.

Well, bless his heart, Leslie didn't say I was crazy. In fact, he didn't say anything right then. He reached over and put his arm around me and I laid my head on his shoulder until "Saturday

Night Live" went off. Then he took me home and I kissed him good night like every Saturday night.

I went back to work on Monday, still thinking about those tapes but trying to concentrate on my job and not get sidetracked again. During the day "Stand by Your Man" came over the store's sound system, and I caught myself singing along. I wasn't singing real loud but I was doing it while checking out Miss Lorena Culpepper's groceries.

Miss Lorena said, "Why, Louise, I believe you like that Tammy Wynette music. You know, I do, too. It got to be kinda mine and Mr. Culpepper's song, you know. I even wanted it sung at his funeral but the children wouldn't have it. They didn't know how often I had reminded myself how much I loved that man even when he'd go off and do some crazy thing or other like not come home for two or three days. It's a powerful song, if you listen to the words. Of course, it takes a voice like Tammy Wynette's to give it real meanin', you know what I mean? You gotta have that little catch in your throat that says your heart's breakin' but it ain't goin' to fall apart 'cause you know no matter where that man's gone he's comin' back home. I felt like that many a time. You'll probably find out for yourself once you and Leslie settle down. Come to think of it, your voice sounds a lot like Tammy's, Louise."

Well, sir, I didn't know how to take Miss Culpepper's comments. Did she mean that Leslie was going to run around on me when we got married? Was he doing that now?

I dismissed all that as just being Miss Culpepper. Everybody said she put up with a lot of Mr. Culpepper's mess when they were married. But the thing that stuck with me was she said I sounded like Tammy Wynette! Nobody had ever told me that before. 'Course, nobody had ever heard me sing a Tammy Wynette song before. There wasn't much call for her songs in church, which was the only place I sang.

I guess right then I decided I was going to give country music singing my best shot. That night I called Leslie and asked him where he got the accompaniment tapes to play on those singalong machines. He said they had some there in the store and he thought they might have some religious tapes at the Bible Bookstore. He didn't know if they had any Tammy Wynette songs at either place.

The next day during my lunch break I went to the Bible Bookstore since it was in the same little shopping center strip as the Piggly Wiggly. They didn't have any Tammy Wynette tapes but they did have some by Sandy Patti, whose picture looked a lot like Tammy's. So I bought a Sandy Patti accompaniment tape of "How Great Thou Art."

I didn't have one of those singalong machines but I figured I could get a feel for how to sing with a tape just by playing it on my stereo at home. I knew all the words to "How Great Thou Art" since we had about sung it to death at church, it being one of Miss Eva Mae Mayland's favorite songs. I put that Sandy Patti accompaniment tape in my portable stereo and prepared to sing along. It didn't take me but a minute to figure out that I might sound like Tammy Wynette but I wasn't even close to sounding like Sandy Patti. I also figured out that the accompaniment I was hearing on that tape didn't sound anything like what Miss Mayland played at church. It didn't even start out with "Oh, Lord, my God." It jumped right in with "How great thou art" and then went in a lot of directions I couldn't follow with a whole symphony full of instruments.

I was somewhat discouraged to say the least. But I figured my mistake was in trying to sing something that wasn't country. I needed a country song accompaniment tape. But I didn't know where to find one.

The next day at lunch I went back to the Bible Bookstore and asked the lady there if she knew any place that carried country music accompaniment tapes. She said she didn't but she thought Miss Grace Meadows, the dance teacher in town, might know. So I called her from right there in the Bible Bookstore. She said she didn't have any tapes herself since she was "not into that country scene" but Marie Bloodworth, the drama teacher at the new consolidated school, might know. I didn't know Marie Bloodworth from Adam's housecat but if she could help me get some country accompaniment tapes I would track her down.

The next day I asked Mr. Washam if I could take the afternoon off to take care of some personal business. To Mr. Washam personal business meant I had some "female trouble" to attend to and I never told him any different. I went out to the new school that had just been built about two miles out of town. It was a big modern building and I had never been there before. I found my way to the school office and when I asked for Miss Bloodworth, the lady there in the office spoke into a microphone that must have been connected to a PA system that went all over the school and asked for Miss Bloodworth to come to the office.

In a few minutes a tiny little lady came into the office dressed from head to toe in black. Her hair was black and she had on a black dress with black hose and she was wearing little soft black shoes. Right off I didn't think I was going to like her because I had never seen anybody that looked like her before. But that goes to show that first impressions can be wrong. She was just as nice as she could be and said she did, indeed, know where I could find some country accompaniment tapes. She said she had worked with the Miss North Carolina Scholarship Pageant for many years and had had occasion "to assist many young ladies in preparing their vocal presentations." It had never occurred to me to think of beauty pageants and country music together. The first thing I thought of in connection with a beauty pageant was girls wearing bathing suits and high heels. Somehow my mental picture of them singing country music in that combination didn't click with me. Anyway, Miss Bloodworth gave me a little catalog that had hundreds of song titles with taped accompaniment. All I had to do was pick out the song I wanted and order it. I thought I had found the answer to my prayers.

That night I went through that catalog and found a lot of country songs. I did not find "Stand by Your Man," however. This being a catalog used for beauty contests, I guess that song was never called for. But I did find "Woman to Woman," a Tammy Wynette classic, and I ordered it. It came in the mail about two weeks later.

I didn't tell Leslie that I got the tape. I thought I would surprise him after I had learned the song. Keeping that information from him proved to be a real test of our relationship.

I sang that song in my mind all the time. I practiced it at home almost continuously. And it was on my mind even when I was with Leslie. A real test came when we were coming back from the football game one night and that song came on the radio. It was all I could do not to sing along with Tammy right there in Leslie's pickup truck.

ON CHRISTMAS EVE, Leslie asked me to marry him. He said it was time. He said that we knew each other well enough to know each other's faults and we still loved each other in spite of it all. He said he wanted to give me everything in the world. All he had was himself, his job, a pickup truck, and a new doublewide, but it was all mine if I'd take it.

He was so sweet I wanted to hug him and kiss him and tell him yes, yes, yes. But I didn't. And I couldn't tell him why, because in the back of my mind I still had this dream of being a country singer and I knew that was not what Leslie wanted his wife to be. So I told him I'd think about it.

"Think about it?" he asked. "Girl, we been thinkin' about it since we was in high school! What's left to think about?"

I could see the disappointment in his face. I didn't know if he was going to get mad or cry. He didn't do either one. We were sitting on the couch there in his doublewide and he hugged me and I put my head on his shoulder like I had done a hundred times before. And I cried.

We kept on going out for the next month like before Leslie asked me to marry him. I was doing what I said I'd do. I was thinking about it. I decided the only way I would ever be able to make the right decision was to try my singing somewhere. One night I asked Leslie if anybody he knew might let me sing for an occasion like a birthday party or something. He said, "As a matter of fact I do. Buddy Hudson is having a pig-pickin' at his place on Saturday night. That's one of those times anybody can do anything and get away with it. I'll borrow a singalong machine and you can try it out."

I was so tickled to know that Leslie was going to help me even after all we'd been through, I near about decided to give him some of that privacy he was always wanting. But I held off.

That Saturday night we showed up at Buddy's place ready to sing. A whole crowd had already gathered. Buddy and his friends had been cooking that pig all day and had drunk enough beer to have floated the pig and its mama all the way to Wilmington.

It was the usual bunch, mostly couples but a lot of singles. When you live in a community like Flynn's Crossing and you've known everybody all their lives you don't have to pair up to get together. Everybody was laughing and having a good time. There was plenty of food. Buddy had cooked that pig just right, and we went by and pulled the meat right off the pig while it was still on the cooker. Then we piled on the baked beans, cole slaw, and potato salad. Most of the boys and some of the girls were drinking beer, but almost everybody had sweet tea with the food.

After everybody was full, Leslie stood up and said, "Listen, y'all. Louise has been practicing to be a country singer. Y'all know there ain't hardly any places around here to practice for that so I thought that tonight, here amongst friends, would be a good time to give it a try. Y'all have heard her sing in the choir but you ain't never heard her sing country. I ain't never heard her neither, for that matter.

"So for just a minute I want you to let her audition for us. Ladies and gentlemen — and you, too, Buddy — please give a listen to Louise."

Everybody got quiet. All you could hear was the top pop as somebody opened up another beer. Leslie had set up the machine and had everything ready to go. I had never even practiced with it. He gave me the microphone, pushed the button on the tape player, and stepped over to the side.

The music started and it sounded like it did on my stereo. When it got to the part where I was to start singing, I sang. I had never sung into a microphone. I had never heard myself on a speaker. I didn't recognize my own voice. But I kept on singing and the more I sang the better I sounded to me. When I finished it seemed like a long time but it really was a few seconds before they all started clapping and shouting.

Leslie came over and gave me a hug and so did just about everybody else. "You bound for Nashville, girl." "I didn't know you could sing like that, Louise." "You sounded just like Tammy Wynette." "Never heard that song sung any better." I heard all that and was so happy I 'bout cried.

Leslie stood beside me shaking hands with everybody as they told him what a great singer I was and how proud he ought to be. He smiled and told them he knew it all the time.

After the pig-pickin', Leslie loaded me and the singalong machine into his truck and we went back to his place. I was on cloud nine. In my mind I started making plans. I was going to find an agent who could get me a lot of "gigs," get me a contract with one of the big recording companies, buy a bus (every country singer's got to have a bus), and start touring the country singing to thousands of people. I told all this to Leslie and he smiled and laughed at how happy I was.

"You're happy for me, aren't you, Leslie?" I asked.

"Honey, if you're happy, I'm happy," he replied.

But something in his answer didn't ring right, although he kept right on laughing and sharing the moment with me as I saw my dream of being a country singer coming true just around the bend. He even brought the singalong machine inside the doublewide and set it up so I could sing again. When we thought we had celebrated enough, he took me home and I kissed him good night. It was a longer kiss than usual.

I told Mama and Daddy about the pig-pickin' and they were excited. But Daddy, being the practical man that he was, said, "How you gonna make all this happen?"

I hadn't thought about that. I just knew that somehow, if it was meant to be, it would. But it didn't happen at all like I thought it would.

ABOUT A MONTH after the pig-pickin', I was over at Leslie's and he said, "I got something for you." He handed me a letter. It was from a recording studio in Charlotte saying they had heard my "demo" and wanted to talk to me. I couldn't believe it.

"That singalong machine can record, too," Leslie said. He had recorded me singing that night after the pig-pickin' when were at his place and sent it to a friend who worked in the studio in Charlotte.

"It don't mean you got a contract or nothin'. It just means they want to talk to you," he cautioned.

It didn't matter. In my mind I had accomplished what I had set out to accomplish. I had become a country singer.

"So have you had time to think about our getting married?" he asked.

I said, "To tell you the truth, I haven't been thinking about it. I been so caught up in all this stuff that's been happening. But I don't need to think about it anymore. My mind's made up."

Leslie's face dropped. He thought he knew what I was going to say. But he was wrong.

"Leslie Carter," I said, "after all these years you don't know me as well as you think you do. I told you I wanted to be a country singer. Well, now I know I am. But every country singer's not famous and every country singer don't make a living singing.

"All I ever wanted was to know that I could do it, to know that it was possible for me to do something if I set my mind to it. And I did. But you know what, I wouldn't ever have known if you hadn't let me try. Not only let me try, but helped me.

"Leslie Carter, you mean more to me than all the applause in the world. There are lots of famous people out there who hear applause and think that all those people applaudin' loves them. While they might love that singer's singing, none of 'em's got a love like I got. You love me while I'm checking groceries at Piggly Wiggly and you love me when I'm singing country songs and everybody's telling me how great I am.

"There's probably a lot of people who would say that I am a fool not to follow up on this singing thing and I may be. I know it may sound corny but I believe I got more real living to do right here in this doublewide than I have on any stage.

"I don't know whether this singing would really amount to anything or not. After all the biggest and only audience I've sung for was my friends at a pig-pickin'! But I know what I've got right here in Flynn's Crossing with Leslie Carter and that's what I'm choosing."

I won't go into what all went on after that, but I will tell you that Leslie didn't give me an engagement ring right away. Instead he ordered a dozen of those singalong tapes and put in a real sound system in his doublewide so I can sing anytime I want to. And now that we're married he's got all the privacy he can handle.

"So he started out the door and instead of sayin' goodbye he said, "Thank you very much." And that's what done it, Ellie. That's when I knew that the man walkin' out of my beauty shop was Elvis. Nobody can say 'thank you very much' like Elvis."

6

A BRUSH WITH ELVIS AT MARIE'S BEAUTY EMPORIUM

I called Ellie the minute he left. I had to tell somebody that Elvis Presley had just got his hair done at my shop right here in Flynn's Crossing.

"Ellie, are you sittin' down?" I asked. Without getting any confirmation from her I went right on with my great news. "I know you gonna say I'm crazy but I'm gonna tell you flat out that I just done Elvis Presley's hair. I mean I washed it, dried it, cut it, combed it out, and sprayed it down. Now before you say another word (which she had not said the first one yet) get yourself over here."

Soon as I hung up the phone I looked around my little shop and started to clean up. Then I thought to myself, "What are you doing, Marie? You are gettin' ready to sweep up Elvis' hair and throw it in the trash can! That hair could be worth millions of dollars! I could put little pieces of it in those plastic sandwich bags and sell 'em for — I don't know — maybe a hundred dollars a bag. There ain't no telling what I might have here. This could be better than selling Avon."

So I left the hair on the floor for the time being 'til Ellie got there. Then I thought about all the other stuff. I had just run that yellow comb through his hair and the sink still had some of the shampoo I washed his hair with. I began to think of all the evidence I had that Elvis had been here and the possibilities seemed endless. I even thought about taking off the doorknob he had turned to get in the shop.

Well, it wasn't too long before Ellie showed up and I opened the door for her so she wouldn't smudge Elvis' handprint on the doorknob. Before I could say anything she said, "Marie, what ails you? I ain't never seen you in such a strut." I told her to sit down in the chair under the hair dryer there and I would tell her the whole story. But first I asked her if she wanted anything to drink and she said she didn't, but I felt like I needed some iced tea so I went over to the refrigerator and poured myself a glass, and added some sugar and an extra-large lemon slice.

So I begun my story, the saga of Elvis Presley's visit to Marie's Beauty Emporium in little ol' Flynn's Crossing, North Carolina, U.S. of A.

I guess the best way to get this story right is to start at the beginning and I told Marie that she knows that I tend to go off on a tangent when I get to talkin' about something so she'd have to keep me focused on the story or I'd never get it told.

Anyway, I had just got to the shop that morning after gettin' my house kinda cleaned up. One of the advantages of havin' my shop right next door to my house is I don't have to drive to work. But the disadvantage is that sometimes I come on over here in my nightgown, particularly if I don't have any appointments scheduled. That was the case this mornin'. I didn't have an appointment scheduled 'til this afternoon when Mildred Cartwright is supposed to get a permanent. 'Course, permanent is not the right world for Mildred's hair 'cause it is fallin' out to the point that she has got a bald spot right on top.

That's when Ellie told me I was beginnin' to wander.

I said she was right I had to get back to Elvis. So I got back on track. Well, I was startin' to sweep up a little bit and I heard a knock on the door. Well, you know don't nobody knock on that door. They just come on in. So I went to open the door and there stood this old man, looked like he mighta been in his late 60s or early 70s. That was the first thing that surprised me. You see, I know that there are lots of beauty shops now that take men customers but mine ain't one of 'em. I always figured a beauty shop was a place where women could let their hair down in more ways than one, and if a man is present the women ain't very likely to talk about some things, like when Gladys told us about gettin' her tubes tied after her sixth child. Now she might have told that if some man was present but she definitely wouldn't have said that the reason she did it was 'cause she didn't know who the daddy was. A man woulda told that all over town, but since she told it here I feel sure that that information never got past these walls.

Ellie didn't say anything but I knew I had digressed so I got back to Elvis. Well, there's this old man standin' outside my shop and he asked if I was open. I guess he asked that since I was standing there in my nightgown and it about half open. I covered up myself and told him I wasn't open yet but I asked if I could help him.

He said he really needed to get a haircut and this was the first place he'd seen since he had just drove into town. Well, Ellie, he looked so lonesome I coulda cried. So I told him to come on in and I'd fix his hair.

He come in and I told him to have a seat in that chair over there, the one that leans back into the sink, so I could wash his hair. Well, he walked over there and sat down kinda slow and easy which, when I think back on it now, was probably the way a man his age woulda moved. You see, at that time I still had no idea whatsoever that he was Elvis.

I turned the water on and laid his head back in the sink. And when I did that I noticed that he had the longest eyelashes I believe I have ever seen on a man his age. 'Course I didn't say anything to embarrass him about it. I just went on and washed his hair. Now, I have to tell you this, Ellie. That man had the thickest gray hair I have ever seen. Usually, you know, when hair starts to turn gray it'll get real brittle and then a lot of it will come out when you wash it. Well, his hair was as thick as a cocker spaniel's and pearly white.

I wouldn't say this to nobody but you, Ellie, but like I said I still had on my nightgown and you know I don't wear nothin' under it. That's part of a deal me and Elroy made when we got married. It saves so much time. But … I know. I digressed again. The reason I mention that is while I was leaning over washing his hair my bosom was completely covered up but it kept swingin' and hittin' him in the face. Well, he was such a gentleman he never said the first word about it. That was my first hint that this wasn't no ordinary man sittin' in my beauty shop.

AFTER I WASHED HIS HAIR I had him sit up and I toweled it partially dry but still wet enough to where I could comb it out. Well, he still had said hardly two words since I put him in that chair. And you know me, Ellie, I can't go no more than a couple of minutes without some kinda conversation so I asked him how he happened to be in Flynn's Crossing. I figured he just happened to be here 'cause don't nobody come to Flynn's Crossing on purpose 'less it's a wedding or a funeral.

He said, "Just passin' through."

I told him I thought he mighta had some family here or something.

He said, "No. ma'am. I've never been here before. Seems like a nice little place though. Reminds me a little bit of home."

I asked, "Oh, where you from?"

"Originally Mississippi, but I've moved around a lot," he replied.

"You in the sales business, I guess," I said.

"No, ma'am. You might say I'm retired."

I looked out the window and saw he was driving an old blue Cadillac. I figured right away he musta been in some kinda business that made him a lot of money at some time or other. I have always wanted a Cadillac but Elroy said the only people that drove Cadillacs was old people and pimps. I don't agree with that 'cause that fella that sells that accidental insurance drives one. I see it every time he comes by to collect the insurance payment. Besides, I only know one old couple that's got a Cadillac and he owns the funeral home, and I don't even know any pimps and Elroy better not.

Ellie told me I was digressin' again.

The man's hair was longish, and I asked if he wanted it cut short or just trimmed. He said, "Just trim it a bit in the back, and comb the sideburns back."

"Now Ellie, it has been awhile since any of the men around here has had sideburns. You remember when we were in high school how Elwood Henry let his grow down to below his ear lobes. Well, that was the way this fella's was. 'Cept, of course, his was gray. Elwood had that jet black hair, you know, and enough Wildroot Cream Oil on it, it's a wonder his cap didn't slip off his head."

I told the man to move over to the other chair so I could blow-dry his hair. He walked on over to that chair there and for the first time I noticed he was wearin' double-knit pants and a pair of those flat-toed boots with the zipper up the side. Elroy had a pair of them 'fore we got married. I used to kid him about always wearin' boots. I told him it was because he never learned to tie his shoes. Elroy didn't think that was too funny, the reason bein' he never has owned a pair of lace-up shoes before nor since.

Anyway, I blow-dried this fella's hair and started combin' it to look like it did when he come in. That's when I noticed again how thick it was. Usually, when an older woman comes in my shop sometimes I can see that her hair has started to thin and I try to talk her into lettin' me tease it some. You know, teasin' hair will make you look like you got more hair than you got and while that's good for folks with thinnin' hair it makes folks with plenty of hair look top heavy.

But the funniest thing happened after I dried his hair. It seemed to style itself. I mean, I didn't even have to brush it. I just run my comb through it a couple of times and it looked fine. I was so surprised I had to say something about it to the man.

He said, "It's been that way all my life, ma'am. My mama used to comb it that way when I was a boy and I never changed it. I guess after all these years that's the only way it can go. Some mighty talented hair stylists have tried but it still stays the same."

So I told him I guessed I had done all the damage I could do and that'd be $10.

Well, Ellie, he took his wallet out of his back pocket and I'll bet you he musta had a thousand dollars in there. He took out a hundred dollar bill and gave it to me and told me to keep the change. 'Course, I told him I couldn't do that but he insisted. So I kept it. Here it is right here. It's probably just as well I kept it 'cause I couldn't have changed a hundred dollar bill anyway.

So he started out the door and instead of sayin' goodbye he said, "Thank you very much." And that's what done it, Ellie. That's when I knew that the man walkin' out of my beauty shop was Elvis. Nobody can say "thank you very much" like Elvis. So I blurted right out, "Are you Elvis?"

He stopped right dead in his tracks. "Oh me, Ellie, that was a terrible thing for me to say. What I mean is he quit walkin' and stood right still but he didn't say nothin'. Then he turned around and walked back in the shop and sat down in that chair right where you're sittin' and he said, 'Ma'am, you wouldn't believe how many times I have been asked that question. I always give them the same answer: No. But there is something about you that will not let me lie again. Yes, I am Elvis Presley.'

Well, you could have knocked me down with a feather. I said, "All these years I been tellin' people you wasn't dead but they kept showin' me pictures of you in a casket and all these people comin' to your funeral. Now, here you are — livin' proof I was right!"

"Yes, ma'am," Elvis said. "But you can't tell anybody. It'd ruin everything. So many people have worked so hard to make everybody believe I'm dead that it would ruin their lives if the truth of my existence was ever known."

I couldn't believe that Elvis had just asked me not to tell anybody he was alive. Ellie, do you know how much *The National Enquirer* would pay me for that information? But how could I ever convince 'em it was so. So, you know me. I never beat around the bush. I just up and ask him how come he set up this big lie.

That's when Elvis went over to the door and locked it and told me to sit in the hair-washing chair. And he began to tell me his story.

HE SAID IT had been Colonel Parker's idea. He had been spending money pretty fast and he wasn't bringin' it in like he used to. And on top of all that his private life had gone to … well, you know. When Priscilla left him he was devastated. He tried getting together with other women but they just weren't Priscilla. 'Sides, Lisa Marie was the most important thing in his life and the Colonel come up with this way of makin' sure that Lisa Marie would always be taken care of. You see, the Colonel said that Elvis was a great artist and all great artists' work sold for more money after they were dead than when they were alive.

So if everybody thought he was dead, he would be able to make more money for Lisa Marie than if he were alive. 'Course, the Colonel would get 50 percent.

According to Elvis, he faked his death and the Colonel and Priscilla made all the arrangements. All he had to do was keep out of sight. That proved to be hard to do as long as he lived in the U.S. of A. So he went back to Germany and lived with Priscilla's folks for a while. But he got so lonesome for home he left and drove all over the country wearin' different disguises. Then one day it occurred to him that there were so many Elvis impersonators that if he was to show up in Las Vegas or Hollywood dressed in his show clothes nobody would think it was really him. So that's what he did.

The only problem was that he started showin' his age and he couldn't even convince the bookin' agents he was Elvis. Money was no problem since Priscilla took over the management of his estate and he was makin' more money than ever and she sent him a check every month. He got to where all he could do was drive around the country like a show-business Lazarus that couldn't die again. The only time he about blew his cover was when Lisa Marie married Michael Jackson. He said that just about killed him for sure. But he said Priscilla told him not to worry about it, that Lisa Marie was goin' through a stage and he didn't have to worry about her since Lisa Marie was too old and a girl to boot. At the time, Elvis said he didn't understand but he trusted Priscilla's judgment.

Ellie, I'm tellin' you, he went on for I don't know how long tellin' me all about his life since his death. Sometimes I thought he was goin' to cry, then he'd go on with his story. I did go into the house and get him a Pepsi once but other than that I just sat there spellbound.

After a while he stopped talkin' and I asked him what he was goin' to do now. He said, "Darlin', I'm going to keep on doing what I've been doing. I don't have much choice. But I tell ya, it's been a great ride if it was to end today. I've had a chance to make up for a lot of the mistakes I made when I was 'alive.' I've seen my daughter grow up and now my granddaughter is getting to be a star, too. They'll never have to worry about money. Priscilla showed the whole world how smart she is just like I knew she would.

"Back when the Colonel had me doing all those dumb movies I went to see a movie one time called *Carrousel*. It was about a fella who had messed up in his life and got killed before his daughter was born but the Lord gave him a chance to come back and see his little girl. I wanted the Colonel to let me do a remake of that movie but the Colonel said that wasn't my kind of movie. But I've always believed that I got to play the part for real."

Well, that's when I 'bout cried. But Elvis got up and started on out to his car, but he stopped in the door there and said, "Now, you can tell anybody you want to that I was here but they're not going to believe you." Then he walked out to that blue Cadillac, got in, and drove away.

So I called you, Ellie. I had to tell somebody. But he was right. Nobody would believe me unless I had some proof. That's why I got to thinkin'. What if we got some of the DNA experts to check out that hair and a fingerprint expert to work on that doorknob? What if we could prove Elvis was here?

Ellie had sat through that whole story without sayin' hardly anything 'cept to keep me on track. But then she said something that made me think that Ellie should have been the valedictorian of our high-school class instead of that stuck-up Myra Murphy. She said, "Would you do that to a man like Elvis?"

And I knew the answer was "no."

❝I knew right then my goose was cooked.

Mr. Dave was not going to give me

a lecture about choices; he was

going to have me arrested for gambling.❞

RANSOM TAYLOR AND THE GREAT MULE RACE

was 17 in the summer of 1938. I'd just finished the 11th grade, the last grade at little Flynn's Crossing School. I had graduated, but I was concerned about my future. I wanted to go to college, but my father was a sharecropper on ol' man Clinton Causey's place, and I knew we wouldn't get enough out of our share of that year's tobacco crop to hardly buy groceries much less send me to school.

I rode with my father into town to sell the lugs, the first cropping of tobacco. We always sold our crop at Mr. White's warehouse. We had worked hard to get that crop ready, been as careful with every leaf as if it was money itself. We had piled the load high in the wagon, the bundles neatly wrapped and placed on the grading sticks. The smell of the cured leaves was what Daddy called "Carolina perfume." We knew that lugs wouldn't bring as high a price as the later croppings but we prepared it just like the rest.

Ol' Jessie, our mule, pulled that load as easy as pie. She didn't even strain, just walked on like it wasn't even there. Daddy was really proud of Jessie. The mule was part of what we brought to the sharecropping deal with Mr. Causey. We prepared the tobacco beds with Jessie, plowed the rows with her, cultivated the fields, pulled the drags from the field to the barns and from the barn to the pack house. Then on Sunday, Daddy would load us all up in the wagon and Jessie would pull us to church. Jessie was more than an animal. She was almost like a member of the family.

We pulled up to the warehouse and unloaded our tobacco, weighed it in, and placed it neatly on circular stacks in a long row. Daddy had promised me a bag of boiled peanuts soon as we got unloaded. I got that and a Pepsi-Cola and sat on a bench outside the warehouse office and listened to the other farmers that had gathered in little bunches.

It didn't help my spirits any.

"Pitiful! Plumb pitiful! I work in the cold of winter and heat of summer to get this crop in and I ain't got enough to pay off the chattel mortgage at the farm store," complained one farmer.

"I don't know what a body's s'pose to do," replied another. "There ain't a whole lot you can do 'sides raise tobacco or run in the logwoods — 'specially for a poor man like me. Won't be long 'fore there won't be nothin' but big farms anyhow."

I heard Mr. White calling for the sale to begin, and the farmers moved toward the line of buyers that were lined up to bid on the tobacco. The farmers followed behind the line, some a row over.

"Listen to that! Tobacco ain't bringin' nothin'! All it's doing is making dishonest men out of us. We got to lie to the folks who holds the notes on the crop, to our wives what want to buy things for the family, and worst of all, we keep lying to ourselves trying to convince ourselves we can make it another year."

"Well, I'm through with it! I'm movin' on. Mr. Kendall can have his little ol' shack back, and I'm movin' on further south. I hear you can make some money in cotton and if that don't work, well, there's always moonshine."

"They lifted prohibition back in '33. Make it harder to make money off moonshine."

"Never happen. Folks has developed a taste for home brew and they ain't gonna give it up even if they can get a taste of the legal stuff."

"Speakin' of taste, y'all goin' to the poker game at Cap'n Henry's barn tonight? Understand Raymond Gautier'll be there to keep the stakes high."

"I believe I'll go. Maybe I can turn this piddlin' amount of tobacco money into enough to get my wife a new dress."

"Yeah, and the whiskey's cheap!"

AFTER I GOT HOME that night I thought a lot about what those fellers had said back at the sale. I set about doing my chores and figgerin' on a way to make enough money to go to school. Much as I liked feedin' ol' Jessie, I couldn't see me spending the rest of my life lookin' at her backside goin' down a corn row.

I walked out to the barn to feed Jessie. I opened the barn door and lit a kerosene lantern, then hung it on the peg next to her stall. I brought her out and poured her feed in the trough against the wall. I didn't even tie her, just let her eat while I began to brush her down.

Then I began to talk things over with Jessie. I always talked to Jessie when I had something heavy on my mind. She never disagreed with me, never interrupted me, and never made fun of me. "Well, girl," I said. "It's just you and me. What kinda pearls of wisdom can you tell me that might get me off this farm and out into the world?"

'Course, Jessie kept on eatin' and I kept on brushin'. "Now, see you got it made, Jessie. You got somebody to feed ya, water ya. Got a dry, warm place to sleep and even somebody to scratch your back every once in a while. Meanwhile, here I am just a good ol' boy with nobody but my daddy to care about me and there ain't nothin' he can do to make things any better. Makes me wonder which one of us is the jackass."

Then I heard a kinda rustlin' sound behind me. It was over in a corner of the barn where the lantern didn't throw much light. "Come on out," I said. "I heard ya." I grabbed up the pitchfork and held it like a rifle. "You better come on out 'fore I start usin' this pitchfork to look for ya!"

Then I saw her. It was Molly Grainger. I had known Molly all my life. She lived about a mile down the road. We had grown up together, gone to school and church together and done just about everything together. I always thought of her kinda like the sister I never had. She was dressed like me with a pair of bib overalls and a denim shirt with the sleeves rolled up, and she had on a pair of brogan shoes.

"Molly Grainger! What do you think you're doin' sneakin' around this barn? Does your mama know you're over here?"

Molly put her hands on her hips and gave me a look like I had never seen from her before. "Don't nobody know I'm over here,

Ransom Taylor. And if you'd put that pitchfork down you could act like you was glad to see me."

I didn't know what to say. This was a side of Molly I had never seen before. "Now, Molly, don't you come over here with none of that mushy stuff. You know I'm a good boy, and you're a good girl and that's the way it's supposed to be, and God will strike us both graveyard dead if we was to listen to the serpent right here in this barn."

"Ransom, I swear you are the beatin'est boy I have ever seen. I didn't come here with 'lust in my heart' for you nor nothin' like that. I might have some news that you'd want to hear about how you could get your money for school this fall. I believe I can tell you more than that mule can."

Then she had that look again, but this time I could tell she was teasing me. " 'Course if you don't want to have anything to do with some girl what might be interested in your body, why, I'll just go on back home."

Then she made like she was goin' to leave. "No, no," I said. "Puttin' your body aside for the time bein', tell me about the money."

"Well," Molly said, still teasing me, "Being the brazen woman that I am, I might need some sort of encouragement that would make me think that at a later time we could consider a more intimate discussion."

"Come on, Molly, quit messin' around and tell me about the money."

"Oh, all right," she said. "I was just kiddin' with ya." Then she got all prim and proper. "Well, for your information, sir, there is a strong rumor that Raymond Gautier is settin' up a mule race this Sunday afternoon down to the paper company road 'long the edge of the swamp. He told my daddy that he'd give $500 to the man whose mule won the race."

I almost shouted loud enough for Daddy to hear me in the house. "Five hundred dollars! That'd do it. That'd get me through the first year at the university."

Then Molly asked the obvious question, the one I didn't want to think about. "Can Jessie run?" she asked.

"Yeah, she can run," I answered. "But I wouldn't exactly call her a racing mule. She can pull a wagon or a plow, but she ain't even in a hurry then, much less runnin'. The only time I ever see her run is when she is headin' toward the barn at feedin' time, and then she can really move."

"Maybe you can train her." That was more of a question than a statement.

"Train her by Sunday afternoon? Are you crazy?" But I thought a minute. "Then again, maybe I can take advantage of her existing training."

Molly looked at me with the quizzical look that she had every time we planned some scheme. "What do you mean 'existing training'?

I put all the negative things out of my mind. The only thing I could see was Jessie crossing the finish line ahead of the rest of the mules.

"Listen, if Daddy knew I had entered his mule in a race he'd kill me. So you got to do it for me. You go tell Mr. Gautier that you'll put up a mule against $500 in the race, but don't tell him who the racer is. If I lose, he gets Jessie. If I win, I get the $500."

"And what do I get?" she asked.

I paused and, without even thinking, said: "A kiss."

"Any chance of advance payment?" she said and kinda smiled at me.

I had already surprised myself with my rash promise so I didn't want to embarrass myself any further. With a sigh of exasperation, I said, "Just go make the bet, Molly."

I SHOULD HAVE KNOWN that nothing can remain a secret in a small community like Flynn's Crossing. The next morning when I went to Mr. Dave's General Store, I should have expected that the front porch crowd would be there to give me a hard time. Just as soon as my foot hit the porch step, Mr. Newt Hall reared back in that rocking chair and said, "Well, well, Ransom, where's your racin' mule?"

"Mornin', Mr. Hall. Ya heard about the race, huh?"

"Oh, yeah," he said expansively. "Word spread all over Flynn's Crossing that we goin' to have a race the likes of which ain't been seen since the Kentucky Derby."

"Yeah, well, I don't know about that," I said. "But I guess it will be the biggest race we've had around here lately anyway."

I could tell Mr. Hall was enjoying the conversation way too much. "Oh, no doubt about that," he said. "Big race'll bring a big crowd to town. Bring lots of money. Take away a lot, too, including a mule." Then he reared back and laughed again.

I was glad to hear Mr. Dave calling me from inside the store. "Come on in here, Ransom, before you give Newt any more fun."

I walked on into the store and the screen door slammed behind me, making more noise than I remembered. I always liked to go into Mr. Dave's store. It smelled of apples and leather, mixed with a little kerosene and candy. It was kind of a haven for me, a place where I could get away. Sometimes I would go out to the feed room and sit on the sacks of feed and think about all the places I wanted to go and the things I wanted to see away from Flynn's Crossing.

"Thanks, Mr. Dave," I said. "But I guess I deserved that raggin'. I believe I mighta messed up good. You know, if I lose Daddy's mule he will never forgive me — if he don't kill me first."

"Well, knowin' all the risks beforehand, why'd you do such a thing?" he asked.

"Stupidity, I guess. No, doggone it, Mr. Dave, I gotta find a way to go to college. You know Daddy can't help me, and I was lookin' for some way — any way — to get up the money to go. Was that so wrong? To want something so bad that you do dumb things?"

Mr. Dave just looked at me. He didn't chastise me for being stupid. "Oh, no, son," he said. "People do stupid things every day for poorer reasons than yours. Some people get married just to keep from being lonesome, and others fall in love and never tell the one they love about it because they are afraid it might be a one-sided deal. Oh, people do stupid things all the time. 'Course, your deal here with the mule race ranks right up there with one of the stupidest I ever heard of." And then he chuckled.

Mr. Dave had not helped me a lot. I was still obligated to race Jessie. "Well, what am I gonna do?" I asked. "I can't back out now, and there ain't no way Jessie can outrun Mr. Gautier's mule. What am I gonna do, Mr. Dave?"

Mr. Dave leaned back on the counter and placed his hands on the edge. I could see where he had poured some fertilizer in the cuff of his pants and ink had stained his shirt pocket. Although it was a hot day he wore a long-sleeve white shirt with sleeve garters.

He said, "Ransom, my boy, in making any decision there are alternatives to take into consideration. One option in this case is to back out and not race the mule — in which case your father would still have the mule that you could plow with until you and the mule die right there on that sharecropper farm. The other option is to race the mule, take a chance on winning enough money to go to college while puttin' your daddy outa business because he couldn't farm with a winded mule, or puttin' your tail between your legs and run on out of town in disgrace."

When he finished, I didn't say anything for a while. Then I said, "Tough choices, huh?"

Mr. Dave went on. "Life is full of tough choices, son. One choice leads right to another, but we keep on making 'em, sometimes stumblin' and fallin' through life. But we have to make 'em, and the best way to decide is to ask ourselves, 'Is this right?' If you decide it's right, then do it and don't look back."

I LEFT MR. DAVE'S a little confused, to say the least. He had not made my decision for me, which was what I wanted him to do. I thought about it all day, and that night I went over to Molly's house and threw little rocks at her window to wake her up.

"Molly!" I whispered as loud as I could. "Molly!"

In a minute I heard Molly raise the window to her bedroom. I looked up and she poked her head outside and whispered loud down to me, "Ransom Taylor, what do you think you're doin'? If you wake up Daddy, your name will be mud!"

"It's not your Daddy I want to talk to," I whispered back. "It's you. Come down here. I got to talk to you."

Molly said, "I can't get out of the house. Daddy always locks all the doors at night, and if I go traipsin' around tryin' to get out I'll wake him up."

"Then jump out the window," I said. "I'll catch you."

In a softer whisper, Molly said, "Do I look crazy enough to jump out of this window into the arms of a boy who ain't much bigger than me?"

I didn't want to discourage her, so I said, "Well, even if I don't catch ya, I'll break your fall. Besides, if you don't jump, we gonna stand right here talking until we wake up your daddy."

I could hear Molly moving around then she said, "What you lack in reasoning you make up in persistence, Ransom Taylor. Here I come, and you better be under me."

Just like she said, I couldn't catch her but I tried. When she hit me I went straight to the ground, and the two of us landed in the hedges that were around the house.

Molly stood up and looked down at me. She brushed the straw and dust off her nightgown, then said, "This ain't ladylike, Ransom, and you the one always talkin' 'bout bein' proper and all."

I ignored her fussin' and said, "Come on. I figured out how we gonna win the race."

I grabbed her hand and we headed across the cornfield toward my house.

I'll never forget that night. Molly and me running across the fields, the moonlight so bright I could see the little beads of sweat on her forehead. The main thing I remember, though, was that somewhere between her house and mine, Molly changed a lot in my mind.

We were running as fast as we could, Molly hasslin' for breath. She let go of my hand and said, "Stop, Ransom, stop. This nightgown wasn't made for racing 'cross cornfields and I'm about to roast in it."

I slowed down and looked back. "Come on. We don't have long."

"Turn your eyes, Ransom Taylor," she said. "I'm rearranging this nightgown. You run on ahead of me."

I didn't feel like arguing, so I ran on. When I got to the barn, I stopped to wait for Molly. When she walked up in the yard, I could see she had definitely rearranged her nightgown. She had tucked the hem of it up in the waistband so that her legs weren't confined. I looked at her, and it came to me that it was the first time I had seen her legs in a long time.

As she walked toward the barn, I realized that the girl who had jumped out the window had been my childhood friend, my confidant, a kind of little sister. But now the girl who stood in front of me that night outside my daddy's barn was a different girl. The evening breeze coming across that field blew her hair and nightgown just enough to make both move. I saw a different girl from the one who had teased me through grade school and counseled me through high school. The vision of this one reached out in the moonlight and stole my heart. Somehow I knew she wouldn't be "Ol' Molly" anymore.

But I was not going to think about that right then. My immediate concern was winning the race. So I blurted out, "Come in here and I'll show you what I'm talking about."

We walked in the barn and closed the door behind us. I could hear Jessie kinda blowin'. Mules don't whicker like horses; they just kinda blow. "Whoa, Jessie," I said. "Just us."

I told Molly, "See how she perks up when we come in. She thinks it's feedin' time."

"So?" asked Molly.

"So if I don't feed her between now and Sunday afternoon she's goin' to be real hungry. That means when she sees feed she's goin' to run to it as fast as she can. Have you about figured it out?"

Molly answered, "You think she'll outrun Gautier's mule if feed is waitin' at the finish line? You know what, Ransom Taylor, you're a pretty smart boy to know so much about mules and so little about girls."

I didn't answer her, but I said to myself, "Mules are a whole lot easier to figure out."

THAT SUNDAY Molly and me took Jessie to the back end of the paper company road down in the swamp. We could hear the crowd before we ever got there. Mr. Hall had been right. There hadn't been a crowd like that in Flynn's Crossing in many years. People brought picnic baskets and some folks were making ice cream, and all in all it was pretty much a festival atmosphere. When I saw Mr. Gautier coming across the clearing, I knew my time had come. Festival or no festival, I had to get down to business.

Mr. Gautier walked up to me and said in that Cajun accent of his, "Well, boy, you be ready for the race?"

I said, "Yes, sir."

"Well, where your mule?" he asked.

I pointed to the other end of the road. "She's down to the startin' line. We didn't want to get her all stirred up and excited what with all the goin's on up here."

"Awright," he said. "It seems that your mule is the onliest mule to challenge my Jake. So, here be the rules. Mr. Dave, he agree to hold the money and be judge at the finishing line. Lit'l Joshua here, he be ride Jake. And Lem Faulk, he fire the gun what start the race. We done measured off half mile. That all the rules there be, boy. First mule cross the line be the winner. You win, I give you $500. You lose, I get you mule.

I had thought there would be more mules in the race, but it didn't really matter. I said, "I think we ought to shake on it."

"You right, boy. Here my hand." And we shook on it.

"Gentlemen," Mr. Dave said, "if you will proceed to the starting line, we'll get on with this race."

Soon as he said that and the crowd saw us walking off, they started cheering. I whispered to Molly, "Now you go stand right behind that finish line with this bucket of corn and keep rattlin' that thing from the time the gun goes off 'til me and Jessie cross the line."

I got down to the other end and got on Jessie's back. Me nor Joshua, who worked at Mr. Gautier's store, had saddles on our mules. We got ready. I kinda hunkered low over Jessie's neck and grabbed the cotton plow lines in both hands.

Lem Faulk got his gun out. I was expecting him to have a pistol, but he had the shotgun he used to go squirrel hunting with. "Awright, boys," he said. "Get ready. Get set. Go!"

That gunshot sounded like a cannon but it didn't faze ol' Jessie. She just jogged on off. But as soon as the gun noise died down, she heard Molly rattlin' that bucket of corn and she began to run.

I was afraid that with all the noise the crowd was making, Jessie wouldn't be able to hear the corn rattlin'. But it didn't seem to matter. She kept on running, picking up speed.

I could hear Molly shouting, "Come on, Jessie! Come on! There's corn aplenty. Come on! Come on!"

Mr. Gautier was hollering, too. "Let 'im run, boy! Put the whip to 'im! Push 'im! Push 'im!"

Molly said, "Come on, Jessie! Come on, Ransom! Please win! Please win!

Then I heard Mr. Gautier plain as day over the noise of the crowd. "The boy's mule is start to falter. Look at 'im! He frothin' at the mouth. Look at 'im! He ain't gon' make it! He down on the road!"

And he was right. The crowd got quiet. I could feel Jessie getting slower and slower but she wouldn't quit. She kept on going even when I pulled back on the lines; she kept on going until she fell in the dirt of the road. She wasn't even breathing hard. She wasn't breathing at all. Her heart had just quit on her.

Molly ran up to me as I sat there in the dust beside Jessie. "Oh, Ransom, are you hurt?" she asked.

"My body ain't hurt, but my heart is," I said dejectedly.

"I did what you said. I rattled the corn. Oh, Ransom, I'm glad you're not hurt," she said trying to comfort me.

But I was beyond comforting. "We lost, Molly. We lost the money. We lost Jessie. *We lost Jessie!* I wouldn't have wanted that for nothin', Molly. She ran her heart out for nothin'. She wasn't no racin' mule. She was my daddy's work mule, and now I've gone and killed her."

I was beyond consolation. This was a calamity of my doing. But Molly kept saying, "It'll be all right, Ransom. It'll be all right. You'll see. Things will work out all right. Besides, I believe two can always do more than just one. Don't you think so?"

The crowd drifted away and Mr. Dave came over and said, "You two go on home. I'll take care of the mule. Ransom, you come to see me at the store in the morning."

THE NEXT MORNING I had about decided I wasn't going to see Mr. Dave. Mr. Gautier had got a dead mule and I hadn't won any money, so I couldn't see any need to go to the store.

But he sent Joshua to get me about 9 o'clock.

I walked in the door and let it hit me in the backside instead of slamming like it usually did. I figured Mr. Dave was really going to give me a hard time about making wrong choices.

He was down at the far end of the counter with a feller I didn't know. Mr. Dave said, "Good morning, Ransom. Come over here a minute. I want you to meet someone."

I walked down to where the two men were. I didn't look at either one, but kept my eyes on the floor.

"Ransom," Mr. Dave said. "This is Sheriff Walton. I believe he has something to say to you about horse racing in this county."

I knew right then my goose was cooked. Mr. Dave was not going to give me a lecture about choices; he was going to have me arrested for gambling.

Mr. Dave went on. "The sheriff seems to think that you were involved in a mule race around here yesterday, but I told him that couldn't be because your mule recently died. In fact, I got him buried in the field behind the store."

"That so, boy?" asked the sheriff.

"Yes, sir. Jessie's sure enough dead. Just worked herself to death," I said. That wasn't really a lie.

The sheriff went on. "Well, somebody had a race over on the paper mill road yesterday, and I arrested this Gautier feller. He had a mule with him all lathered up, and he had over a thousand dollars in his pocket. Now, after some talkin' he told me that he had that money to set up a scholarship for boys who wanted to go up to state college to study agriculture and improve the breed of mules around here and he give me this money."

The sheriff waved that money like it was a handful of wilted flowers. A thousand dollars would be enough for me to go on to school and buy Daddy another mule.

Mr. Dave spoke to the sheriff in a real serious tone. "Sheriff Walton, I happen to know that young Ransom here has had just such plans. Do you know of any other young people in this county with similar ambitions?"

"No, sir, I don't," was the answer.

Mr. Dave went on. "Well, as magistrate of this township I would like to submit the name of Ransom Taylor for your consideration."

The sheriff looked at me and said, "Well, based on that recommendation and the fact that nobody else has applied for this scholarship, I guess you can have the money, boy. Come by the office sometime next week and we'll take care of the paperwork." Then he winked at Mr. Dave and said, "See ya later."

I didn't know exactly what to do. I kinda figured what had happened, but I was afraid to admit it for fear it might undo the deal. So I said, "Thank you, Mr. Dave. I know you're behind all this."

"Let's just say it helps to know the right people," he responded. "Now, I want you to go off to that school and make something of yourself. We need good folks in Flynn's Crossing, and I believe it's a good place to raise a family. And I happen to know a young girl that agrees with me."

It's been a long time since all that stuff happened. Been a lot of memories of Flynn's Crossing — hot tobacco warehouses, old men spittin' on wooden porches, mules racing down a dirt road and people urging them on. And then there's the memory of the girl in the flannel nightgown with her damp hair blowing in the moonlight.

We got a little girl named Jessie.

"" In the dry places … towns, like weeds,
spring up when it rains, dry up when
it stops. But in the dry climate the husk
of the plant remains. The stranger might
find, as if preserved in amber, something
of the green life that once was there
and the ghosts of men who have gone
on to a better place. The withered
towns are empty, but not uninhabited. ""

— Wright Morris, The Works of Love

8

THE HOMECOMING

I had not been back to Flynn's Crossing in almost 30 years. After Mama died, I just couldn't make myself come back. I wanted to remember it like it was when I was growing up. I didn't want to see it change. I knew it would, though. It had been the center of the farming and logging community, and when those two endeavors began to shrink so did Flynn's Crossing.

But more than anything, it had been where Rabon, Jackson, Terri, and I had grown up. We all do that, you know. Grow up I mean. Some people always think of something in their growing up that they would change, but I can't. Up until we all graduated from high school, ours had been a perfect world.

We were inseparable. We all lived within a couple of blocks of each other. We were in each other's yards and houses indiscriminately when we were little. Jackson and Rabon and I had played football and baseball together in high school. Terri was a cheerleader. But even if we didn't have a cheerleading squad for baseball, she'd come to every game and cheer us on. She tried to get on the team one time, but that was before girls were allowed to play. She would have been a good player, too. She'd always been kind of a tomboy. She would do anything the other three of us would do. We did everything together and we had no secrets from each other.

I probably would have come back to Flynn's Crossing some time, but I was coming back this time for a sad reason. Jackson had died and I was to be a pallbearer at the funeral along with Rabon and Terri. Jackson had told the doctor before he died that he wanted Terri to be a pallbearer, too. Nobody was surprised about that.

But there was a surprise. Jackson's will left everything he owned to the three of us. Jackson had gone to Vietnam after high school. Then when he got out, he came back to Flynn's Crossing and opened up a service station/garage, one of the few of its kind anymore. The reason it was such a surprise that he left it all to us is we had not seen each other in nearly 30 years. He had done really well with his business although he continued to live in a little apartment above the station. He never married.

So when we got the call from Mr. Turner, the attorney who was handling his estate and taking care of the funeral, we were all a little surprised. Jackson had died from complications resulting from his time in Vietnam. It seems he had been sick for quite a while, and he had taken time to plan out everything. That was just like Jackson — organized and methodical. He was our leader, the one who usually made the decisions after we had discussed everything. I was the nerd of the group. They called me "professor" and teased me about always being so serious. I had gone on to college the fall after we graduated, became a teacher, and had been teaching high school in Raleigh ever since.

Rabon was the happy-go-lucky one. He liked building things, and he liked anything to do with the outdoors. He had inherited his uncle's farm just south of Fayetteville, added to it, and was a very successful farmer.

Terri was "Miss Energy." She was always doing something, never still and never taking life too seriously. She was also the peacemaker. On those rare occasions when any of us had a serious disagreement, she was the one who would mediate. She had become a nurse and married a doctor in Wilmington.

We had drifted apart, never realizing just how separate our lives had become. Now we were all back together, all four of us, almost strangers.

AFTER THE FUNERAL we all went to Jackson's apartment over the service station. Mr. Turner had already told us that the will was pretty simple. We owned everything jointly. When we met at the apartment it was the first chance we had had to think about what we were going to do.

I was the first one there. Mr. Turner had given me the key, so I went on in and was looking around when the others showed up. It was a simple but nicely furnished little place. The furniture was spare but good quality. A big leather sofa and recliner faced a giant-screen television in the living area. There was a bedroom off to the side, and a kitchen area that was part of the living room. It was the kind of place we could picture Jackson living in. On a shelf were several trophies acknowledging Jackson's high-school athletic achievements. There were also some medals commemorating his military service. There was a picture of the four of us in our caps and gowns the day we graduated from high school.

None of us spoke at first. We just looked around and then gradually took a seat. It was Terri, the most outspoken one, who asked the question we all had in our mind. "Why did he do this?" We knew she meant, why did he leave the business to us?

The question got no response.

Finally, it was Rabon who broke the gloom. "You know, he must have had a reason, but I know he wouldn't want this to be a sad time. That wouldn't be like Jackson. Remember he was always the practical one, never doing anything without a reason. Do y'all remember the last time we were all together, that summer after graduation? That was one of the happiest times of our lives and I'll bet that's the way he would want us to be now."

For the first time since we had been back in town, a smile came on each face as we remembered that time. Our whole senior year we had planned how we were going to celebrate graduation. We decided to take two canoes, one of Rabon's and one of Jackson's, and the four of us were going to go down the river as far as we could in one day. That was to be our great adventure — one that would seal our friendship forever.

As we began recalling that trip — each remembering bits and pieces — the sense of excitement seemed to come back as if it were yesterday.

WE HAD STARTED PLANNING the trip one Sunday night after church revival. Really, it was while the service was going on.

We had all slipped out of the building during the songfest that began each night's service. We went behind the church fellowship hall and I remember Terri pulling out a cigarette.

"When did you start smoking?" I asked.

"Tonight. I saw those commercials where everybody's sitting around the campfire smoking and drinking beer. I figure I better learn how before we go on the canoe trip."

"Are you crazy, girl?" said Jackson. "There ain't going to be no cigarettes and sure ain't gon' be no beer drinkin' on our trip. We got to stay focused. Keep our wits about us. That river's tricky and we gotta be alert. 'Sides, you ain't never drunk any beer in your life. One can and you'd be drunk as a skunk."

"You don't know everything, Jackson Piner. I drank some of Homer Johnson's beer down at the beach last summer."

"Well, did you take a likin' to it?" he asked sarcastically.

"To tell you the truth, it tasted terrible. But I didn't let him know that. Nobody's going to say Terri Prosper couldn't hold her liquor — even if it was half a can of beer."

I remember we all laughed at the idea of considering half a can of beer a test of liquor capacity.

"You can forget the cigarettes, too," Jackson said. "Them things'll stunt your growth, and little as you are you don't need any help in that area."

We all knew better than to question Terri's ability to take care of herself despite her size. "I may be little but I can whip your sorry behind, Jackson Piner," she said, then laughed realizing that she was just posturing, knowing that Jackson was big and strong enough to pick her up and carry her if he wanted to.

We finally got around to talking about what we would need for the trip but didn't finish our plans before we heard the congregation singing the "hymn of invitation." That's what the preacher called it when he wanted people to come down the aisle and give their souls to the Lord. That was something all four of us had already done, and we figured we didn't need to do it again, not having but one soul to give. Anyway, we decided to continue our plans later.

We finally got all our plans laid out, so when the day after graduation came we pretty much had our mess together. Jackson was the only one who had his own vehicle, a 1958 Ford pickup he had bought for just about nothing and fixed up himself. Early that morning we loaded all of our stuff in the back and tied the canoes across the cab. Jackson said if we turned the canoes sideways we'd look like Flynn's Crossing's version of the Wright Brothers' airplane. Jackson and Terri got in the front and Rabon and I got in the back, all of us happy as larks.

It was about 9 that morning before we got to the river. We unloaded our stuff, carried the canoes down to the bank, loaded them, and set off down the river. Jackson and Terri were in one canoe and Rabon and I were in the other. The sun had come out bright and warm and with the current pushing us along, we didn't have to do much paddling.

Rabon and I were in front of Jackson and Terri. Nobody was doing any talking; we were just enjoying the scenery and the feeling of being on a great adventure together.

After a while I heard Jackson holler at us, "Y'all watch when we get to Clayton's Ferry and don't run into that cable that guides the ferry."

Rabon and I just nodded. We knew about the ferry as well as Jackson did. There had been some Sunday afternoons when the four of us would get in Jackson's truck and go down there and ride across. It wouldn't carry but about four regular-size cars. After we'd get the truck on the deck, we'd get out and stand next to the railing letting the wind blow on our faces and hearing only the pumping of the ferry engine.

Thinking about those times made me look back at Terri and Jackson. Terri looked like she did on the ferry when the wind would blow her hair and she'd be smiling like she was in love with the world. I wondered then why she still hung around with us guys when every other boy in school wanted to take her out. Even for the junior-and-senior prom we all went alone and stood around the punch bowl together. A lot of the other guys would ask Terri to dance and she would, but she also would make each one of us dance with her at least once. She said we needed to learn how to dance so we could progress in the social world.

I was thinking how pretty she looked at those prom dances as I watched her paddle the canoe down the river. It occurred to me about then that Jackson and Rabon and I had been about the luckiest boys in Flynn's Crossing. I began to think that all those other guys had envied us and our special friendship with Terri. We had taken for granted a friendship that they all wanted. It never crossed our minds to think of Terri as anything other than one of us, maybe like a sister. But as we quietly eased on down the river, I began to think about what we had shared and for the first time realized it was all about to change.

About the time we got to the ferry, Rabon said we ought to stop there and eat our lunch, so we did. You could tell we had each packed our own provisions. Jackson, Rabon, and I had Pepsi-Colas to drink and Terri had a Cheerwine. Jackson had a MoonPie and a bologna sandwich. I had peanut butter and jelly and four Oreos. Rabon had a can of Vienna sausages and a banana flip. Terri, bless her heart, had a ham, lettuce, and tomato sandwich and a slice of her mama's nine-layer chocolate cake. We all thought we were feasting there on the banks of the river.

WHEN WE FINISHED OUR MEAL, we got back in the canoes and headed on down the river. Everything was going along fine until we got to where the river forks. Right about there the current picked up some. I don't mean it was like rapids or anything, but we didn't have to do much paddling. Rabon said all the rain must have made the rivers flow a little faster and when the two came together it made the current stronger. Whatever the reason, we were moving along at a pretty good clip, and Rabon and I were concentrating on keeping our canoe balanced and watching out for debris that had accumulated and might hit us.

I looked back to see how Jackson and Terri were doing, but I didn't see them. I told Rabon we ought to pull over until they caught up. That was not easy to do, but we were almost to the bank when Rabon decided to reach up and grab a tree limb that was sticking out. When he did, the limb hit him in the head and he fell out of the canoe. I saw him swimming, so I knew he wasn't badly hurt. I got the boat to the bank by myself and went back to where he was.

"That was about the stupidest thing I have ever seen," I said.

"Well, I seen 'em do it in the movies and thought I'd try it.

Musta stood up too soon or something," was his reply. Fortunately, it was a hot day and the dunking cooled him off a little. We sat down to wait for Jackson and Terri.

But after about 30 minutes they still hadn't shown up, and we began to worry. "You reckon something happened to 'em?" asked Rabon.

"Must have," I said. "But I didn't hear 'em holler, and Jackson's the best at canoeing there is."

"We ought to go back and see if we can catch sight of them," Rabon suggested.

"Yep," I agreed. "It's going to be dark soon, and we hadn't planned on being on this river at night. But we'll have to walk through the woods. There's no way you and me can paddle upstream in that current."

The wind had begun to pick up a little, and I could tell we were about to get one of those summer showers. Sure enough, in a few minutes we heard a bolt of thunder and the rain came down, soaking us. Or, I should say, the rain soaked me because Rabon was already soaked.

We kept on walking, stumbling over fallen tree limbs and slogging through marshy areas. Every few minutes we'd call out, "Jackson, Terri, can you hear us?" but the rain hitting the leaves and our own walking noise made it impossible to hear a response even if they made one.

The shower ended about as quickly as it began, and we kept on walking, calling, and looking out to the river for any sign of Jackson and Terri. We walked for an hour or more, and the sun was starting to go down. Rabon and I were exhausted, but we couldn't stop.

Just as I thought they might have disappeared, Rabon shouted, "Look, there's their canoe!" He pointed out to the river. Indeed, it was their canoe. Empty. We both slumped to the ground, our eyes following the canoe until it floated out of sight.

"They're goners," said Rabon. "That current's too strong."

His words echoed my thoughts, and I was suddenly very weary. The thought of them drowning on what was supposed to be one of the happiest days of our lives was too ironic. I cried, not a whimper but great sobs. I cried not only for the loss of my friends, but because there was nothing I could have done to save them. I wished I could have drowned with them.

Rabon was crying, too, and in my sorrow I felt compelled to confess my deepest feelings. "I loved her, Rabon. I never cared about the other girls because they couldn't compare to Terri. Now she's gone." And I cried some more.

It seemed to me that without her I might as well end my own life. There was no reason to go on. I stood up, tears still rolling down my cheeks, and started walking out into the river.

"Billy Ray, what are you doin'?" Rabon shouted.

I didn't respond, just kept walking. I fully intended to be swept away like Terri and Jackson, joining them in some glorious continuation of our youth.

"You idiot, you'll drown in that river! Get your sorry butt back up here!" Somehow through my grief and misery, I determined that the voice was not Rabon's. It was Terri's.

Given my recent self-pitying condition and overbearing sorrow, you would think my first reaction would have been great joy. But not me. My first thought was, "Oh, my God, did she hear me say I loved her?"

I turned around and saw the three of them looking at me. I didn't say anything, just starting walking back. I was thinking, "Should I ask her if she heard me?" My immediate answer to myself was, "No. If you ask and she didn't hear you, then she'll want to know what you said."

Another question came as a shock to my by-then-befuddled mind, "Did Rabon tell her what I said?"

When I reached the bank Jackson and Rabon pulled me up. "I was just going out farther in the river to see if I could see y'all," I said with great stupidity.

Then Terri said something that I had sometimes thought myself. "To be the smartest boy in our class, you do some of the dumbest things."

Jackson, ever the pragmatist, said, "Come on. We got to get off this river before it gets dark."

We started back to where our lone canoe rested. Jackson decided it wouldn't hold all four of us, so we were faced with deciding who would go back in the canoe and who would trek off through the woods to the nearest road. Although the canoe might have held three of us, nobody wanted to leave one person alone to get through the woods.

Again, Jackson, our leader, made the decision. "We'll leave the canoe. Let's all start walkin'." So we did. Jackson said since the river ran southeast, we ought to head northwest because we would run into a highway, which meant our back would be to the sun. Only there wasn't any sun. There also wasn't much land. It was a lot of marsh to start with; then gradually we got to higher ground. And before too long, sure enough, we came out on the highway.

We didn't try to thumb a ride, but a man driving an old stake-body truck picked us up and took us to a gas station where Terri called her father to come and get us. After seeing that we were all right, he really got on us boys about taking his little girl and "putting her in harm's way." We didn't say anything. Finally, Terri said, "It was my decision to go, Daddy. They didn't drag me off. Besides, we're all right and we accomplished what we set out to do."

Mr. Prosper acted like he couldn't believe what she was saying. "What you set out to do? You set out to almost drown yourself in the river? I don't believe that was your goal!"

"No, Daddy. Our goal was to have an adventure that we would always remember, and I guarantee you that we'll never forget this trip."

SHE WAS RIGHT, of course. As we sat there 30 years later in Jackson's apartment, the memory was still so fresh on our minds. As we recalled the story, the years seemed to slip away; we were 18 again and the world was ours for the taking. Recalling and sharing the emotions of that day re-created the bond that had almost vanished with the passage of time.

I thought to myself that once again Jackson had been the leader of the group. In making us come back for his funeral, he had led us to remember who we were and that special time of our lives. He gave us back that memory of optimism that had faded as we all faced the realities and struggles of our adult lives. We began to recall other adventures that we had shared and began to laugh as we remembered.

We turned the disposition of Jackson's business over to Mr. Turner, who rented it to a big oil dealer in Wilmington. He said he would mail rent checks to us once a year, but we decided to come back to Flynn's Crossing and pick them up personally. That way we would never lose touch with each other again. I'll bet that's what Jackson had in mind.

After taking care of the business in Mr. Turner's office, we all headed to our cars to go back home. We hugged and said we'd see each other next year. When I hugged Terri, she whispered, "I heard what you told Rabon on the riverbank that day." Then she kissed me on the cheek and drove away.

66 As the camel walked into the scene, Miss
Lundstrum was so startled by the sight
of the big animal, she fell off her stool.
Not ever having seen an animal like a
camel, the donkey started braying and
kicking, the cow's eyes got big with fright,
and the two of them pulled the stable posts
down … the sheep took off down the street
along with the milk cow and the donkey. **99**

HERD IT AT FIRST BAPTIST'S NATIVITY SCENE

Every year I say I'm not going to do it again, but I do. I promise myself and my husband that I will not direct the live Nativity Scene at the church during Christmas. It is a losing proposition for everybody. My husband winds up having to get involved in the livestock part of it, and he is not a country boy. My children have played every role because I can't find anybody else to do it. And inevitably I catch a cold from being out in the night air so much.

But every year when the preacher asks for volunteers and no one else will do it, I "get volunteered." Oh, everybody says, "We'll all help you, Louise." Bless their hearts, they do try; but honestly, sometimes I'd just as soon do it without their help. The whole thing is supposed to bring out the Christmas spirit, but

I'm telling you right now, I will not do it again unless the Lord speaks directly to me and says that directing that pageant is my key to heaven.

The reason I am so adamant about this thing is the way this year's pageant went. It started off bad and went downhill from there. Right after the Thanksgiving service Reverend Ashby came by the house that Sunday afternoon and begged me to do it again.

"Louise," he said, "You have a great talent for this. It is a God-given talent that you should use for His glory." I thought that was really stretching it a bit given that the past live Nativity Scenes had not been glorious by any standard.

I was determined to turn him down. I said, "Preacher, God has given me so much and I am thankful for it. I can sing, but He never put me on stage at the Met. I like to paint a little and I've even won some local art shows, but you don't see my stuff hanging in any gallery. I'm even a pretty fair shot with a rifle, but Mama didn't name me Annie Oakley. So, talent or no, I don't feel God calling me to direct this pageant again. If I was good at it, God would have had me producing on Broadway."

Then he got past the flattery and spiritual coercion and cut right to the nitty-gritty. "Nobody else will do it, Louise, and it would be a real shame if we didn't have a Nativity Scene. It is a part of this church's tradition."

Guilt is a powerful sword in the hands of a preacher. So I reluctantly agreed.

I didn't tell my family until two nights later at supper. "Louise, I absolutely refuse to be responsible for any more animals," was

Richard's response. "My leg still hurts from where that donkey kicked me two years ago, and I will never live down James Clayton telling me that goat was a sheep and everybody laughing at me. If you are bound to do this, find somebody else to take care of the animals. That is my final say on the subject."

Jana, my daughter who is now 16 years old, said she was not going to be in it again. She said everybody kidded her last year when she played Mary to Mackie Wishon's Joseph. "I won't even go into all the insinuations they made about what kind of baby me and that nerd would have. It was not something you tell your parents about."

J.R., my 10-year-old son, was the only one who seemed to want to help. "I'll help, Mama, if I can be a wise man. I've never been a wise man 'cause you always said I was too short, but I checked with Miss Ellen at Sunday school and she said there was no place in the Bible that said the wise men were tall."

Jana, the ever-supportive sister, said, "There weren't any midget wise men, either."

I HAD EXPECTED that kind of reaction, but I also knew that when I got down to really needing somebody, my family always came to the rescue — even if reluctantly. So I went ahead with the preliminary activities needed to get ready for the pageant.

Fortunately, I didn't have to worry about costumes. We had accumulated enough robes and head coverings to clothe Bethlehem. Over the years we have had so many different size people that we have finally reached the point that there should be a costume to fit anyone. Some of the clothes, of course, may be in better shape than others. I knew that some of them would have to be cleaned, especially the one the wise man was wearing last year when he slipped in the sheep pen on his way to place his offering at the manger.

I would have to make a new crown for one wise man. The only one we had on hand was a tiara that Georgia Martin had let us use. It was the one she won as Miss Tomato Queen almost 20 years ago and she wanted it back. Maybe she needs it to remind her of what she looked like 20 years ago.

Most of the other costumes were in pretty good shape. After the pageant last year I personally hung each of them on hangers and placed them in the storage room in the fellowship hall. I went down there on Monday morning to gather the ones that would have to be washed. I wound up with about 15 items. I was probably the only person who knew they were costumes. Off the rack and piled on the floor of my laundry room they looked like a big pile of bedsheets.

After placing them all in the washer, I sat down to try to come up with a cast. Like other churches we would have auditions, but inevitably there would be some roles that nobody wanted. Unlike a regular Christmas pageant, a live Nativity requires more than one person for each role since everybody can't be present every night that the scene is being presented.

The angel chorus was always tricky casting until I came up with the idea of recorded music a few years ago. The regular choir members said they just couldn't sing every night, so I always had to find some substitutes. Now, I don't care whether they can actually sing or not because they will sound like the Mormon Tabernacle Choir. The same thing applied to the narrator. I got Joe Harris down at the radio station to read the narration and put it on a cassette along with the music; so all I have to do is push a button on the tape player and let it go. There are some disadvantages to this that I'll tell you about later.

WE HAD THE AUDITION the next Sunday afternoon. J.R. wound up being a shepherd again. I had convinced the deacons to take turns being wise men. I only needed about four shepherds per night, but I could only get two other boys to agree to play the role so J.R. had to be there every night. Plus, I convinced April Woodard, who was in J.R.'s class, to be a shepherd, explaining that once she put on her costume no one would know she was a girl. That was more to satisfy J.R. than April. J.R. said his Sunday school teacher said there were no girl shepherds in the Bible. (I had begun to appreciate the patience of J.R.'s Sunday school teacher.)

I had no trouble finding Mary and Joseph for every night except Friday. Friday nights are basketball nights at the high school. Attendance, if not participation, in that activity takes precedence over sitting in a Nativity Scene for two hours if you are a teenager in Flynn's Crossing. Finally, in desperation, I got Miss Amy Lundstrum — who is creeping up on 82 her next birthday — and Mr. Luke Howard — a wonderful old gentleman who lost his wife last year — to be Mary and Joseph on Friday night. By covering their heads with the hoods from their robes, nobody would be able to tell their age.

On every night but Friday, the Adams twins, Elizabeth and Joanne, alternated as the angel Gabriel. Mildred Aft, the church organist, substituted on Friday night. They stood on a platform right behind the shelter and among some tall myrtle bushes along with the choir so they looked like they were floating in air.

So I had the casting pretty much done, but I still didn't have the animals. This is really what makes the Nativity Scene "live," but it is also the most difficult to control. Richard still refused to be in charge of the animals, but he did agree to help get them to the scene.

Homer Haslette let us have four sheep, which we put in a little pen right beside the shelter where Mary and Joseph were seated. He also had a donkey that he let us borrow, and we tied him to the post that held the shelter up and put plenty of hay right at his feet so he would be contented enough to stand there and eat. Miss Alvi Jenkins let us tie her milk cow to the post on the other side, and we gave her plenty of hay, too. (The cow, not Miss Jenkins.) All in all, I thought it would go well.

That's when I should have let well enough alone. J.R. was really getting interested in the biblical accuracy of the Nativity so he pointed out to me that the real wise men had camels. He said if we were going to show people what it was like when Jesus was born, we had to have camels. I pointed out to him that there were no camels readily available in Flynn's Crossing. He asked me if I would put some in the scene if he could find some. Having lived here all my life, I knew the chance of finding a camel in this part of the country was slim to none.

So I foolishly agreed.

I am not well acquainted with computers, particularly the internet, but J.R. is. With his internet expertise he somehow found a man in Raleigh who rents camels. You wouldn't think there would be enough market for rented camels in North Carolina to justify such a business but evidently there is. As J.R. informed me, this guy has a kind of backyard zoo and rents animals for parties and such. J.R. said we were really lucky to find this camel because Christmas is the height of the camel-renting season. Having acquiesced to his request to put the camel in the Nativity Scene if he could find one, I had no choice but to agree to the rental of the camel.

So we added a camel to the Nativity Scene. Of course, J.R. told everybody he came in touch with about the new addition, and it created a lot of interest. I began to have people ask me at the grocery store about the camel. Because of J.R.'s creativity and insistence on biblical accuracy, we were expecting a big turnout for the week of the presentation.

We had a simple rehearsal on Sunday afternoon before officially opening the scene on Monday. It went relatively well. Of course, we didn't add the animals since they would be more or less static. Raymond Wadsworth had a few problems with the sound system but he worked them out, as did Jimmy Winkler with the lights. The lighting and sound were really simple. There were floodlights on the manger scene and one spotlight that came on and went off in accordance with the appearance of the angel and/or the angel choir. Raymond had run a long extension cord for the sound system out to the scene and Jimmy plugged his lights into it.

About 6 on Monday night I went down to the church to start getting everybody in place with a quick dress rehearsal just to check the sound and lights and to make sure all the animals were in their proper places. Everything was fine except the camel had not arrived. J.R. was a little anxious. He was the one who had arranged for the camel and his "reputation" — I never did figure out what for — was at stake. When the camel wasn't there by 7, J.R. called the man in Raleigh to find out the problem. It seemed that the camel had come down with some sickness and would not be there that night. Needless to say, J.R. was absolutely devastated. The man, however, promised J.R. that as soon as the camel was able to travel, he would be there.

J.R. never asked how the man was to determine the ability of a camel to travel, but he took the man's word that he would show up sometime before the week was over.

EACH NIGHT THAT WEEK we waited with great anticipation for the appearance of the camel, but he didn't show. For some reason, maybe because we had done it so many times before, the presentation went well each night. The only hitch came on Wednesday night when Natalie Fuller came to tell me that she had a sore throat and would not be able to sing in the chorus that night. I told her that her sore throat really wouldn't hamper the performance because all the music was recorded. She persisted, however, in the need for her to leave the church. I saw her drive off with Josh Bentley a little while later. Some parts of our youth never change.

By Thursday night J.R. was almost in tears. Some of his friends had begun to tease him and call him "camel boy." Seeing his son embarrassed to the verge of tears brought out Richard's fatherly indignation. Friday morning he got on the phone and called the man in Raleigh and threatened to sue him for breach-of-promise if the camel didn't show up that night — sick or well. I was really proud of Richard. He is in the retail shoe business and wouldn't know how to file a breach of promise lawsuit if his life depended on it, but he bluffed the camel owner into promising to be there Friday night.

Friday night came and all was set for the last night of the Nativity Scene on the church lawn. As planned, the various substitute cast members were there ready to take their places. The music began and the narration followed, first with the prophecy by the angel followed by a song from the choir. Then to the accompaniment of music, Mary and Joseph walked to the stable leading the donkey. (We had tried to put Miss Lundstrum on the donkey, but she couldn't balance herself by sitting sideways on the little animal's back and she said "ladies do not ride astride.") While Mr. Howard, as Joseph, tied the donkey to the stable post, Miss Lundstrum, as Mary, took her place beside the manger and placed the doll in it. (I was a little amazed that J.R. had not had some question about why Mary would have the baby somewhere else, then take it to the manger.)

Still no camel.

The angel choir appeared above the myrtle bushes and sang a couple of songs; then the shepherds came into the light of the stable. They all knelt down, but I could see J.R. kept turning his head toward the church parking lot expecting the camel to arrive at any time.

We had one little glitch during which we had to shut everything down while Mr. Howard left the scene for a few minutes. Age has its own requirements that cannot be halted regardless of circumstances.

Again there was a long narration followed by more choir music and more narration regarding the arrival of the wise men. Right then I saw the headlights of a truck in the parking lot. The camel had arrived! It was almost too late, so I went over to Raymond and told him to rewind the sound back to where the choir was singing and before the narration about the wise men. That would give us a little time to get the camel in place. I had to tell Leo Fowler, the deacon/wise man who was to lead the camel, to get ready.

By then everybody else had seen the truck arrive and was looking toward the parking lot. But the music kept playing and I could see this huge animal emerge from the back of the truck. It lumbered down the wooden plank onto the concrete, and I could see a man pulling on the camel trying to speed him up as Richard ran along beside. But the camel only had one speed: *slow.*

Eventually, the camel got to the edge of the Nativity Scene and Leo took the lead rope from the camel owner, and he and the other wise men began walking into the floodlit scene. And that's when it happened.

As the camel walked into the scene, Miss Lundstrum looked up and was so startled by the sight of the big animal wavering over her she fell off her stool. Not ever having seen an animal like a camel, the donkey started braying and kicking, the cow's eyes got big with fright, and the two of them pulled the stable posts down causing the whole thing to collapse. The sheep pen had been anchored to the stable post; subsequently, with the collapse of the pen the sheep realized their lack of confinement and took off down the street along with the milk cow and the donkey.

Everybody checked to see how Miss Lundstrum was. She was fine. The shepherds had ducked out of the stable as soon as the ruckus started, so they were safe. For some unexplained reason, Raymond and Jimmy kept the sound and light going. So among all the chaos was heard the angel choir singing "Glory to God in the Highest" as people rushed all over the place. All through the whole mess the camel just stood there, his head held aloof as if asking what all the fuss was about.

I DID THE BEST I could to calm everybody down and to make sure nobody was hurt. Fortunately, nobody was injured. I did notice that Mr. Howard was being especially comforting to Miss Lundstrum, so I didn't worry about her condition.

I was very worried, however, about J.R. and Richard. I had not seen either one since the camel came on the scene. I started asking if anybody had seen them, and finally somebody told me they had seen them running down Main Street after the animals. I got in my car and went to find them.

Flynn's Crossing's main street is not much as main streets go. But that night it was unique in that on one corner a donkey was tied to a telephone pole and farther on a milk cow was calmly walking down the middle of the street in front of Miller's Grocery. The scene was made even more unearthly because there are no streetlights in Flynn's Crossing, and the scene created by car lights shining on out-of-place animals made me think I was in a Fellini movie.

I kept on going down the road through the middle of town because I had discovered a trail of sheep droppings, not something you ordinarily see nowadays even in rural towns like Flynn's Crossing. Shortly, I saw several small lights in a field that ran beside the Holiness Church. I figured it was the men trying to catch the fleeing sheep.

I parked the car by the side of the road and began to walk out toward where all the lights were shining. In a few minutes I could make out some talking. "Go over that way, Leroy, but don't move too fast. We don't want to get 'em running again."

Then another voice said, "If we can get them over to that fence we can work 'em down to the gate and we'll just leave 'em in Jackson's pasture 'til tomorrow."

If I thought the scene of the animals back in town was surreal, the sight I saw in that field was plain unnatural. There were several men with flashlights walking slowly in the darkness. Every once in a while I would catch a glimpse of a man in a shepherd's robe grasping the hem of the garment in one hand and a flashlight in the other. After about 20 minutes, they had herded the sheep into the pasture and started walking back toward town. I put as many as I could, including Richard and J.R., in my car.

Nobody spoke a word. I don't think anybody was angry or sad or even disappointed, just tired and overwhelmed by all that had transpired.

I stopped the car to let two of the deacons out to catch the cow and untie the donkey to get them back to the church and the stock trailers they came in. When they had gotten out J.R. said, "Mom, if Bethlehem had been anything like Flynn's Crossing, Jesus would never have been born."

I have half a mind to direct the Nativity Scene next year just to see what will happen.

“ Listen, Ervin, if you want to be mayor
of Flynn's Crossing, theoretically all you
got to do is say you are mayor. Since
there's no town council or any other
legal entity to remove you from an office
that doesn't exist, you'd be the mayor. ”

10

THE MAYOR
OF FLYNN'S CROSSING

Ervin Bowman announced he was going to run for mayor of Flynn's Crossing. Naturally, he made this announcement down at Vila's Diner where just about everybody whose wife doesn't cook breakfast comes to eat. In most other towns such an announcement would be news but not especially noteworthy. But in this case it was most unusual because Flynn's Crossing doesn't have a town government. In fact, we are not even incorporated. According to Mr. Lem Hampton, we were incorporated way back about 1900 or something, but the big mills let it go out of incorporation so they wouldn't have to pay municipal taxes on top of county property taxes.

But Ervin didn't let a technicality like that keep him from running for mayor. He said this town needed some representation in the county. He said nobody paid much attention to our needs and he thought he could get that attention.

John Canton, who happens to be the county attorney but lives in Flynn's Crossing, pointed out the futility of Ervin's effort. "There is no legal entity to represent, Ervin," John told him. "To what government body would you represent the people of Flynn's Crossing?"

"I would represent the people of this town — the people of Flynn's Crossing who have as much right to be heard as anybody in the big towns," was his reply.

We could see that John was getting a little frustrated trying to explain things to Ervin. "There is no such thing as a mayor of an unincorporated town. A mayor's main responsibility is to preside over meetings of the town council. We don't have a town council. The town council makes the decisions that are in the best interest of the people they are elected to represent."

"And if there ain't no town council then the mayor will just have to do it himself," Ervin replied.

Seeing that it was useless to continue the discussion, John left to go to his law office. The rest of the breakfast crowd then looked to Ervin to see if he had changed his mind or had any further explanation for his decision.

Ervin took their silence as a sign that they had understood his explanation for running for mayor. "Okay, now that that's settled, who wants to run for vice mayor?"

By that time everybody had seen that Ervin was determined to go on with his political quest. So they uniformly and without further disparagement decided to go along with Ervin to see what he would do.

"The first thing I'm going to do is have a rally. That'll give me a chance to present my platform to all the citizens and to show them that I am the best qualified candidate for the office of mayor," Ervin declared.

"Who's runnin' against you, Ervin?" asked Leroy Simpson with a little chuckle.

"Well, nobody yet. But whoever decides to take me on better be prepared to lose," he said. He felt the urge right then to let his fellow citizens know that he had the fire of his forefathers burning in him. So he launched into the kind of rhetoric he felt they expected from him. "I've been living in this town since I was born. I know the needs better than anybody and I'm willing to do whatever it takes, pay whatever the price, make whatever sacrifice is needed to make this town the envy of all who live here and elsewhere."

With that the breakfast group broke into applause, then immediately left the café. The rest of the day the whole town was talking about Ervin's foolish candidacy.

"If he wants to run for something to represent the folks around here, why don't he run for county commissioner?" asked Kenny Lacky.

"'Cause he probably knows he can't beat old Lester Cooley," Jake Fuller responded. "He's been commissioner for at least 20 years what with filling unexpired terms and all. Ervin knows good as you and me that Lester's got a lifetime lock on that job if he wants it. It would be a waste of time and money to run against him."

"Well, if this running for mayor ain't a waste of time and money, I don't know what is," laughed Kenny.

THAT WAS ABOUT the tone of the conversation all over town when folks got to talking. Some were amused, some were puzzled, and some thought Ervin must have lost his mind. But none of them realized just how serious Ervin was about this campaign.

The first thing Ervin did after he left the breakfast meeting was go over to the board of elections office at the county seat. He walked right in and told Helen Goldman, the secretary, he was there to file for the office of mayor of Flynn's Crossing.

Helen thought he was joking and said, "Ervin Bowman, I ain't got time for your foolishness. Now what did you come in here for?"

"I come to file for mayor of Flynn's Crossing," he repeated.

Helen was a humorless woman. Her husband had been killed at the Battle of the Bulge, and appreciative veterans had got her appointed secretary of the board of elections, and she had held the job ever since. She had survived all kinds of political shenanigans, and through it all folks had learned she didn't put up with any shady politics (if she knew about it) and she took her job seriously.

So Ervin's request was not taken lightly by Helen.

"First of all, Ervin, there is no office of mayor of Flynn's Crossing to file for. Secondly, even if there was — and I repeat, *there is not* — the date for filing for any municipal office has already passed. Your only recourse at this point is to be a write-in candidate; but that, too, is impossible since no such office exists."

For the first time, Ervin had no immediate response. He looked at Helen and she stared back at him. After a while he said, "What if such an office was created. Could there then be a write-in vote?"

"If there was a duly constituted election for that office then I suppose you could be a write-in candidate, yes," she replied. "But you don't have a municipal government in Flynn's Crossing, Ervin. To have an election the people who are to be represented have to agree to be governed by an elected body duly recognized by the State of North Carolina. The people in the town have to agree to be incorporated, and included in that incorporation process is the organization of a governing body."

The whole situation was getting too complicated for Ervin. The only thing he knew he wanted was to be mayor of Flynn's Crossing. "How would all that start?" he asked.

"Well, the people could petition the state for recognition through the county, I guess. But that takes a long time, Ervin, and you'd have to get a lawyer to handle the process."

Clearly, Helen was going way beyond the scope of her office and her knowledge so she said, "Listen, Ervin. If you want to be mayor of Flynn's Crossing, theoretically, all you got to do is say you are mayor. Since there's no town council or any other legal entity to remove you from an office that doesn't exist, you'd be the mayor."

Finally, Ervin had an answer to his question. He left Helen's office and went over to Luther's Print Shop. Ervin and Luther had known each other all their lives, gone to church together and all through high school together. Ervin found Luther wrapping some newly printed flyers for the local Piggly Wiggly.

"Hey, Ervin. How are you, my friend?" was Luther's greeting.

"I'm fine, Luther. Listen, I need you to print me up some flyers that say 'Bowman for Mayor.' Can you do that for me pretty cheap?"

Luther had heard about Ervin's campaign and decided to go along with what he considered the fun of it all. "Sure thing. In fact, I'll print 'em up for you and consider it a campaign contribution."

"I appreciate that, Luther. Now, don't do anything fancy. I don't want folks to think this is one of those expensive campaigns. Lord knows we've had enough of them. In fact, I'm probably not going to have any other kind of advertising except word of mouth, of course.

Television and radio ads are a little beyond my means. If you could, though, I'd like for you to print 'em up as soon as possible. I want to get 'em out before the big rally next Saturday."

Ervin's next stop was at the volunteer fire department. One volunteer fireman was always on duty; that day it happened to be Eli Coleman.

Ervin walked right in while Eli was washing the new fire truck. "Eli, y'all got anything scheduled here next Saturday?"

"You mean like a fire?" said Eli with a laugh.

"No, no. I mean like any kind of fund-raising. Y'all are all the time having something to raise money to buy a new fire truck or something. You got anything next Saturday?"

"Well, no, we ain't, Ervin. What you got in mind?"

"You reckon I could have a political rally here? I need a place for people to come and listen to my speech. You know I'm running for mayor of Flynn's Crossing."

"Yeah, I heard about that. I reckon it'll be all right for you to have your rally here. You know, the county fire marshal says we can't be partial to any political party since we get money from the county but since there ain't nobody runnin' against you ... well. Anyhow, I really ought to ask all the volunteers or at least Yancy since he's the chief, but I'll say it's all right unless they tell me different."

Ervin thanked Eli, got in his truck and drove to the Flynn's Crossing Methodist Church.

That's where I came into the picture. I'm the pastor for that congregation. Like everybody else in town, I had heard about Ervin's campaign, but I wasn't expecting to be involved. Preachers, other than maybe Billy Graham, are hardly ever associated with politics and Reverend Graham is certainly nonpartisan.

Ervin knocked on the door of my study and I let him in and asked him to have a seat. He seemed somehow ill at ease, a condition I had never seen him in before. "What can I do for you, Ervin?" I asked.

"Well, preacher," he said. "It's like this. I've kinda taken on a project that I really need your help in. I'm kinda embarrassed to ask 'cause, you know, I'm not a member of this church or anything. But you are the one I believe I can call on."

I was a little flattered that this man would call on me to provide him with spiritual support in his effort. "I heard about your running for mayor, Ervin. I think that's an honorable thing you're doing. Wanting to help your community is really a way of showing how much you care about your fellow man. I wish more people who run for political office would seek God's wisdom. If you'd like, I'll be glad to pray here with you right now and ask God's blessing and guidance."

"Well, I'd appreciate that, preacher, but what I really need from you right now is about a hundred folding chairs. Eli Coleman told me I could use the fire station for my rally this Saturday, but they don't have any chairs down there, and I know that y'all got plenty here 'cause I was here for homecoming back a few months ago and there was plenty of chairs for everybody. I'd like to borrow 'em for Saturday. I'll take good care of 'em and get 'em right back to you before church Sunday morning."

Without knowing it, Eli had taught this preacher a lesson in humility. Of course, the folding chairs had been lent out to many family reunions and other gatherings, so the request wasn't so unusual. The church policy, however, was that only members could borrow the chairs and even then we had to get permission from the social committee and that was, essentially, Miss Ida Price.

So I began to try to tell Ervin diplomatically that I couldn't lend him the chairs. "Well, to tell you the truth, Ervin, our church committee of which Miss Ida Price is the chairman has to make that decision. The committee usually relies on Miss Ida's discretion and you know Miss Ida, she's awfully particular about things."

Before I could continue my excuse, Ervin said, "Oh, I know Miss Ida real well. She was my teacher in the eighth grade. If you think I need to ask her I'll sure be glad to do that. In fact, I'll run on down to her house right now and see if I can catch her at home."

He immediately stood up to leave and said, "By the way, preacher, when you were offering to help get the Lord involved in my campaign, well I want you to know what a wonderful gesture that was and how much I appreciate it. In fact, if you still feel so inclined, I wouldn't mind if you would ask Him to help me out in this thing. Everybody always needs the Lord on their side."

Whereupon Ervin left in his truck headed for Miss Ida's. I thought to myself, "If he thinks he needs prayer now, wait 'til Miss Ida gets through with him."

A FEW WEEKS LATER Miss Ida related to me the story of Ervin's visit. As he intended, he drove directly from the church to Miss Ida's house. Miss Ida had retired from teaching eighth grade many years ago, but she was still very much a teacher. If you were ever one of her students, you would always be one of her students even if you got a doctorate in philosophy from Duke.

Miss Ida greeted Ervin at the door and asked him into what she referred to as her "parlor" where she instructed him to sit on the sofa. She asked if he would like a cup of coffee or a glass of iced tea. Ervin politely declined and began to state his business. Miss Ida then sat down in the wingback chair with the floral print.

"Miss Ida," he said, "the preacher down to the Methodist church said you were in charge of letting people borrow the folding chairs from the church, and he said if I wanted to borrow them for my rally Saturday I'd have to get your permission."

"And what kind of rally might that be, Ervin?" she asked. Miss Ida was not one to spend a lot of time listening to other people's conversation so she had not heard about Ervin running for mayor.

"I'm running for mayor of Flynn's Crossing, and I'm planning on a rally down at the fire station Saturday to let everyone know why I'm running, and I need to borrow the chairs for the crowd to sit on," was his simple, straightforward reply.

"Well, Ervin, I never knew you had any interest in public service. I also didn't know that we had a mayor's office in Flynn's Crossing. How do you propose to win this nonexistent seat?"

Ervin then went through the whole business that Helen Goldman had told him about over at the board of elections. Miss Ida did not interrupt his recitation. When he had finished, she stood up and moved over to sit beside Ervin on the sofa. She reached out and took his right hand in both of hers and said, "In all my years of living in this community, I have never seen such unselfishness. You propose to run for an office that doesn't exist, much less pay anything, solely because you want to do something for your community. Ervin, that is the pure essence of America. That is the concept on which this country was built and which, unfortunately, has been ignored for so many years by those who would seek some personal embellishment from public office. You are rare indeed, my boy."

Miss Ida told me that she was so overcome with emotion that tears came to her eyes. She told Ervin how proud she was that he had been one of her students, mediocre as he was. Then she told him he could borrow all the chairs he wanted, and she called me right then to tell me. I figured Ervin must have done some praying of his own between the church and Miss Ida's house.

Ervin spent most of the day Wednesday putting up his flyers all over town. At prayer meeting that night, I had to struggle to get the congregation to stop talking about Ervin so we could have the meeting. Afterward, some of the ladies came up to me and said they wanted to talk about Miss Ida lending the church chairs for Ervin's rally.

"First of all, he's not a member of this church. Secondly, Miss Ida must be getting senile. And, thirdly, she does not officially have the authority to lend these chairs. It is a committee decision."

I said, "Ladies, Ervin talked to me about borrowing the chairs. I referred him to Miss Ida. If you have a difference of opinion with Miss Ida, I suggest you take it up with her."

Of course, that was the end of the discussion. I knew none of them had the guts to face Miss Ida. They had been her students, too.

SATURDAY WAS A BEAUTIFUL DAY. The sun was shining, and it was just cool enough for folks to wear a jacket or sweater. Right after lunch I went by the church office to check my telephone messages, then went on down to the fire station. What I saw was amazing.

Everybody in Flynn's Crossing must have been there. As I walked up to the crowd I saw Reverend Bailey, the new minister at the

A.M.E. Zion church. We had already become acquainted, and as we shook hands I commented on how surprised I was to see such a crowd.

"I'm not," he said. "Did you know that Ervin came by my church Wednesday night to speak to my congregation and ask them to come to his rally? That is the first white person to come to that church since I've been there. No, sir, I'm not surprised to see this crowd."

There was a long table set up outside the door of the fire station. In keeping with the Southern tradition of providing liquid refreshment at political rallies, Ervin was providing plenty of sweet iced tea. Miss Ida was pouring.

Ervin had prevailed upon little Jimmy Southard and his band to come out and play a little bluegrass. This was their first public performance. Their sound equipment also provided Ervin with a microphone when it came time to make his speech. The band sat on one end of the body of a flatbed trailer that had been pulled up outside the station. The borrowed church chairs were placed in front of it. They were all occupied and there were a lot of folks standing up. The doors of the fire station had been rolled up, and folks were sitting in there or leaning against the fire trucks waiting for Ervin to begin.

The candidate himself was walking around shaking hands with everybody. And I mean everybody. He shook hands with the women and the children and every man he could get to.

He kept saying, "'Preciate y'all comin'," over and over.

After he had shaken every hand he could reach, Ervin took the stage. The band quit playing, and Ervin walked up to the microphone.

The speaker squealed a little, Jimmy adjusted it, and Ervin began. He spoke like he had done it a hundred times before, not like the novice he surely was.

"I truly do appreciate y'all coming out here today. I know most of you are here out of curiosity to see how big a fool I'm going to make of myself. I'm wondering about that myself. But just the fact that all of you showed up for this thing is the reason I said I wanted to be mayor of Flynn's Crossing.

"I have lived here near 'bout all my life except for the time I spent in the Army, and I can tell you I wouldn't want to live anywhere else in the world. I know most of y'all feel the same way. But, you know, sometimes we get to takin' things for granted. Especially each other."

Ervin then paused a little while and there wasn't a sound to be heard. Everybody was listening. And that's what he wanted.

"When I came back from Vietnam there was not a parade or anything like there had been for my daddy when he came back from Germany in World War II. In fact, hardly anybody said anything at all about the war, good or bad. Kinda like you didn't care.

"I found out you did care, but what you cared about was me, not the war. You took me back into this community like I'd never left. You let me help coach the Dixie Youth baseball team. You elected me a deacon in my church — the church I grew up in. You bought the insurance policies I had to sell. You made me a member of the Lions Club. And, yes, you let me join that elite discussion group that's held every morning down at Vila's. You let me be as much a part of this community as I wanted to be. Somebody said one time that, 'a small town is a place where people care about you whether you want them to or not.' Well, that's the kind of place Flynn's Crossing is.

"Now, I know I been talkin' about runnin' for mayor of Flynn's Crossing, and I've learned that I can't do that since there is no such office. But today I'm here to declare that there is such an office. It's a one-man, unofficial position and I'm going to take that office 'cause I got no opposition. Now, the real reason I wanted y'all to come here today was not to rally me into office. What I really wanted you to do is look around and share with each other what a special place this is. I figured if I could get you all together in one place at the same time, you'd feel like I do. You are special people. You make up my hometown and, by golly, I'm now the mayor. I'm going to get one of those identification cards and wear it on my coat pocket so everybody will know I'm from Flynn's Crossing 'cause I'm proud of it."

When he stopped talking there was a long silence; then everybody started clapping and Ervin walked into the crowd and started shaking hands again. And everybody else started shaking hands with each other. I was proud to be from Flynn's Crossing myself.

Well, that's how Flynn's Crossing got a mayor. We still aren't incorporated. We still don't get the kind of attention we ought to get from the county office. But we got us a mayor and we got each other.

ABOUT THE AUTHOR

BORN AND RAISED IN HALLSBORO, Bill Thompson graduated from Campbell College (now Campbell University) with a degree in English. Having lived most of his life in southeastern North Carolina, he has worked as a teacher, a television-show host, and an entertainer. He has served as master of ceremonies for countless festivals, celebrations, and beauty contests and is a popular speaker throughout the state.

Most of Bill's professional career, however, has been spent furthering the cause of the Boys and Girls Homes of North Carolina, a statewide, nonprofit organization that provides year-round residential care for children ages 10 to 18 at Lake Waccamaw. Having first come to work for the organization in 1966, Bill was elected president in February 2003.

For more than 20 years, Bill has amused readers of various newspapers in the Carolinas with tales, observations, and reflections on life in North Carolina. Since 2001, the Columbus County native has delighted readers of *Our State* magazine with his warm, folksy column "Front Porch Stories." In 2003, Our State Books released Bill's first book, *Sweet Tea, Fried Chicken, and Lazy Dogs: Reflections on North Carolina Life*, in which Bill further explores his down-home roots through lighthearted commentaries and short stories that celebrate rural and small-town life in North Carolina.

Bill and his wife, Linda, make their home in Hallsboro. His daughter, Mari, lives in Charlotte. His son, Will, resides in Whiteville, just a few miles from Hallsboro. When he's not on the road or writing, Bill enjoys riding horses, singing in the church choir, and savoring his daily classic Carolina snack — a Pepsi and a pack of Nabs.